I0611115

LOVECRAFTIAN

THE SHIPWRIGHT CIRCLE

CALIBER®
BOOKS

By Steven Philip Jones

Bushwhackers
The Clive Cussler Adventures: A Critical Review
Comics Writing: Communicating with Comic Books
Henrietta Hex: Shadows from the Past (with Shannon Denton)
Lovecraftian: The Shipwright Circle
King of Harlem
Sherlock Holmes on the Air (with Matthew Elliott)
Talismen: The Boy in the Well (with Barbara Myers)
Talismen: The Knightmare Knife (with Barbara Myers)
Wizard's Academies: The House with the Witch's Hat

LOVECRAFTIAN:
THE SHIPWRIGHT CIRCLE

&

HERBERT WEST – RESURRECTED:
"THE EMPTY HOUSE ON HARLEY STREET"

By
STEVEN PHILIP JONES

BASED ON CHARACTERS & SITUATIONS CREATED BY
H. P. Lovecraft

INTERIOR ILLUSTRATIONS BY
Trey Baldwin

COVER ART BY
Manthos Lappas

CALIBER BOOKS / DETROIT

Copyright © 2019 by Steven Philip Jones

"The Empty House on Harley Street" © 2015 by Steven Philip Jones

Interior illustrations © 2019 by Trey Baldwin

Cover illustration © 2019 by Manthos Lappas

First Edition

"The Empty House on Harley Street" was originally published in *Reanimator Tales: The Grewsome Adventures of Herbert West & Supernatural Horror in Literature.*

For additional information visit the Caliber Comics website: www.calibercomics.com

No part of this publication may be reproduced or transmitted in any form or by any means, electronic or mechanical, including photocopy, recording or any information storage and retrieval system now known or to be invented, without permission in writing from the publisher or specific copyright holder, except by a reviewer who wishes to quote brief passages in connection with a review written for inclusion in a magazine, newspaper, website or broadcast.

To S. T. Joshi
In Respect and Gratitude
S.P.J.

Yet for each dream these winds to us convey,
A dozen more of ours they sweep away.

- H. P. Lovecraft, XIV. Star-Winds, *Fungi from Yuggoth*

I do believe that Eblis hath
A snare in every human path
- Edgar Allan Poe, *Tamerlane*

"Looking back is a bad habit."
- Charles Portis, *True Grit*

Make friends, make friends, however strong
    Or weak they be:
Recall the captive elephants
    That mice set free.
- *The Panchatantra*

ARKHAM

Massachusetts

Map adapted from works by Lovecraft and subsequent authors of the Cthulhu Mythos

POIs Story-specific locations Roadway Railway River

0   500 Feet

0   100 Meters

N

Bolton, Ipswich

Old White Stone

The Dark Ravine

Ipswich, Innsmouth

Ravine Lane

Old Chapman Farm House

Arkham Sanitarium

Dyer St.

Derby St.

Dr. Nathan Shrewsbury

Curwen St.

Toe Sargent Bus Stop

Federal St.

Noyes St.

Halsey St.

Brown St.

Jenkin St.

Gedney St.

Hyde St.

Marsh St.

Square

Whateley St.

Asbury H.E. Church

Salem, Boston

Armitage St.

Arkham Advertiser

High Lane

High Alley

Manchester, Gloucester

Arkham Station

Water St.

Water St.

Aylesbury St.

River St.

Miskatonic River

River St.

Dunwich

Wooded Graveyard

Main Street

French Doctor

Hangman's Hill

West Church

Town Hall

Christ Church

East Church

French

Boundary St.

N.W. Peaslee

Church Street

Burying Ground

Baptist Church

Hill

Crane St.

Miskatonic University Quadrangle and Campus

Lich St.

St. Mary's Hospital

College St.

Garrison Street

'Witch House'

Parsonage Street

Walnut St.

Peabody Avenue

Orne's Gateway

East St.

Hill St.

West St.

Pickman St.

High Street

Daniel Upton

Albert N. Wilmarth

Powder Mills St.

French Hill St.

Sentinel St.

Saltonstall St.

Miskatonic Ave.

Washington St.

Kingsport, Salem

Christchurch St.

Christchurch Cemetary

Hangman's Brook

Arkham Map courtesy of David Bayer

CONTENTS

ILLUSTRATIONS

All Interior Illustrations by Trey Baldwin

Cover Art by Manthos Lappas

Abdul Alhazred has no one to blame for all that happens next.

CHAPTER ONE

MEMORIES & POSSIBILITIES

1

Abdul Alhazred is running for his life.

Never once does he turn his head to look back, knowing if he does he might spy the awful something pursuing him.

But what is pursing Alhazred goes unseen by the hawkers and patrons in Samarra's crowded marketplace, though they hear it and sense it and recoil from its reek.

Abdul Alhazred also knows he has no one else to blame for all that happens next.

For being hoisted high off the ground and his life sucked out.

His body crumpling gray.

Turning brittle.

And collapsing to ash without a flake touching the earth.

A single breeze carries away the stench as cautious bystanders approach

2

"Abdul Alhazred fled Damascus for Samarra in 738 AD."

It is the gloaming of the vernal equinox, but the drapes in the study of 66 Pickman Street, Arkham, Massachusetts, a two-storey square Georgian house, have been drawn since dawn. Randolph Carter, a tall young man with professorial features, feels inspired at night, so he counterfeits the sable divinity with threadbare long curtains and pale light from a tarnished green-shaded library lamp whenever he must work during daylight.

"A poet, scholar, and indifferent Moslem, Alhazred worshipped hidden, hideous entities with names like Yog-Sothoth and Cthulhu. After a ten-year pilgrimage to supposedly demonic nameless places in the Rub' al Kahli and Al-Dahna deserts, he dared to write *Al Azif*. Several Samarrans claimed to have watched the ghastly price Alhazred paid for that effrontery."

Carter's study has wide floorboards, handcrafted wall shelves, and Adam-period mantle. Furnished with heirloom antiques that—with the exception of a carefully preserved Underwood typewriter—have seen better days, his workstation is his grandfather's corner desk. Modern necessities such as the personal computer, printer/copier/scanner, and landline telephone are secondhand and at least a decade old. Standing out as an almost garish anachronism is a 1965 GE console phonograph with AM/FM tuner and a reel-to-reel tape recorder Carter uses to play ambient music or sounds whenever his habituation is insufficient to mask the tinnitus that has plagued him since he was nine. Scrolls and maps and codices and books and newspapers and magazines are scattered everywhere. A time-eaten Latin grimoire with what looks like a leathern cover lies open beside Carter's elbow as the young man dictates into a handheld microcassette recorder from handwritten notes on a legal pad.

"In 950 A.D. Theodorus Philetas of Constantinople translated *Al Azif* under the title *Necronomicon*, and for a century it reportedly impelled certain experimenters to terrible attempts, when …"

Rapping at the front door interrupts

Carter closes the grimoire. "Who's there?"

"It is I, Pickman! Let down your hair, Rand-puzel!"

A sigh of relief, then quietly: "Blast you, R.U." Louder but no steadier: "Hang on." Carrying the grimoire to a tall Elizabethan chest, Carter stashes it in a lockable drawer, empty except for an aromatic wooden box carved with Gothic grotesques and bound in rusty iron with its own formidable lock. Carter drops the drawer key in with several others in a replica first-century bronze South Arabian bowl on a Victorian hall tree in the foyer before opening the door.

Richard Upton Pickman, SoHo handsome in conspicuously casual bohemian wear, smiles at his childhood friend. "Bathrobe for daywear? Playing Auguste Dupin again are we?"

"Why are you here?"

"Truly? You don't know what's happening?"

"I've been working all day. What's wrong?"

Pickman slides his head back and forth.

"What?"

"You always think something is wrong."

"You've never been a half-glass-full person yourself."

"That's beside the point. Get dressed and let's go."

"Why?"

"You'll see."

"I can't come out and play right now."

"Why not? Warren isn't going to be any less impressed with you if you give yourself a break and take one, so let's go."

Carter wants to argue but succumbs to curiosity. "Fine."

"Great!" Pickman starts to enter.

"Wait here." Carter closes the door.

"Hey! It's cold out here!"

"*Severe prohibentur.* You don't have clearance."

Pickman leans against the threshold, not bothering to disguise his frustration. "Seriously?" Then, to himself, worried: "For what, *le chevalier*?"

3

A young woman smiles at Arkham's Witch House.

The seventeenth-century First Period with saltbox roof has looked spryer. Three formidable gables facing front droop, hoary clapboards sag, and missing weathered shingles dot the roof, but the woman notices none of these blemishes, preferring to concentrate on a long boarded up third-storey window facing north towards the corner of Pickman and Parsonage Streets.

The front door opens.

An elderly man with a laborer's sturdy but stooped posture steps out followed by two unremarkable college students, one of them shaking the old man's hand, excitement kindling his eyes. "Thanks again. I really do appreciate you letting me reserve my room for next year, Mr. Banaczek."

"An old Polish proverb says it's easier to spend money than expectations."

Frank Elwood, the shorter, more pedestrian of the students, draws: "Such logic borders on irreducible complexity ... unless, of course, Gilman vulcanized his check."

Walter Gilman backhands his pal's gut. "Don't listen to him, Mr. Banaczek. I often wonder if Frank could find his wallet with a metric tensor."

Banaczek shrugs. "Smart men do adore big words. Men like me? We're satisfied if we simply don't outwit ourselves."

Elwood: "Another Old World proverb?"

"Common sense, I hope. Good night, boys." Banaczek backs inside to shut the door as the students stroll towards Parsonage.

Gilman is delighted.

Elwood is befuddled. "What are you thinking? Paying six month's rent in advance?"

"'Everybody has three mortgages these days.'"

"Six months! Just to stake a claim on a moldy, misshapen ... "

The woman appraising the Witch House transfixes Elwood.

"That's not misshapen." Elwood approaches the smartly dressed gal with Bette Davis eyes. "Pardon me, but do you live here?"

Without bothering to redirect her attention: "You don't want to go there, boy."

"Don't get me wrong. I only ask because my buddy just rented a room and -- "

Redirecting her sights on Gilman: "Did you now? The Witch Room?"

Elwood groans, acquainted with her tone of voice. "Oy. Another one."

"Another 'what'?"

Gilman beams. "You know about Keziah Mason?"

"This is east Massachusetts. Everyone knows about Mason and Brown Jenkins."

Elwood: "Ah, yes. Bay Staters are already locking up their children in dread of May Eve."

"*Walpurgisnacht,*" Gilman corrects without thinking.

"Sure thing, fan boy." Conceding he is drilling a dry hole, "Let's motate. I bet we can still catch the second half if we hurry."

The woman scrunches her eyebrows. "'Half' of what?"

4

"The Miskatonic Shipwrights are on the brink of making history!"

Students, faculty, employees, and patrons unaffiliated with the university roar at the flat panel high-definition televisions positioned inside The White Ship Tavern.

"If Jackson Carter makes his third free throw, Miskatonic will be up by one with fewer than three seconds left."

The world seems to hush.

On the televisions: "Carter readies ... it rims out!" The crowds on TV and in the tavern howl. "The Wildcats recover ... Uthoff fires from half court ... miss!" Crowds cheer. "We're headed for overtime!"

Pickman stands to exchange high fives with anyone, he doesn't care whom.

Carter sits at their tiny circle corner table. "When did you become a basketball fan?"

"I'm a fan of the moment." Pickman downs the rest of his stepping razor blade and then whispers, "Any chance you're related to that player?"

Carter knows Pickman knows better. "You're a fan of *this* moment?"

"Naturally. It's potentially unprecedented. Such moments don't cross your path every day."

"Unprecedented doesn't necessarily equate to significance."

"This one is. No First Four team has ever defeated a number one seed to progress to the Second Round of the tournament."

"So the announcers have made abundantly clear. What they fail to explain is the purpose of it all. Its significance."

A new voice: "Does something have to have a purpose to be significant, Dolph?"

Pickman and Carter welcome Edward Derby, flaxen with sapphire eyes and boyishly handsome enough to look two years shy of thirty rather than forty. Wedging their way through the crowd behind Derby are the man's unofficial older brother Daniel Upton and Upton's wife Dinah, who asks, "Permission to join you sophists?"

"Better ask Randolph if you have clearance." Carter ignores Pickman as the Uptons squeeze in beside him and Pickman pries, "I'd have thought you'd be watching this with Eddie," referring to the couple's eight year old, Edward Derby Upton.

Dinah takes her husband's hand. "His school is in on Easter Break, so he's in Bolton visiting my folks. It's been calm, but we're adjusting." Tomboy pretty and wearing casual earth-toned rustic fashions that compliment her tawny skin and russet hair and eyes, Dinah, the associate director of the university's admissions office, is almost two decades younger than Upton, an architect with a striking resemblance to Hoagy Carmichael. "So, what were you two boys quarrelling about this time

Pickman: "Randolph and I never quarrel. We debate."

"Of course. My mistake."

Carter: "I don't understand why R.U. is so enthusiastic about this pointless event."

"Because the moment is potentially unprecedented."

"It's only unprecedented because of the rules of a game, not because of an event in nature. If you ask me, you're getting carried away, permitting aesthetics to overrule your metrics."

"'Aesthetics'? I'm a painter!"

"I know you're an artist, but when have you been a Romantic? Richard Upton Pickman is a thorough, painstaking, almost scientific realist."

Derby: "One who aches to stir the dormant sense of strangeness in humanity's latent instincts or hereditary memories."

Pickman: "Precisely! Good Lord, Randolph, even this poor man's Baudelaire sees it. Peel thy peepers! Unprecedented moments are by their essence strange. Rather our team progresses or not, just look at the communal response the anticipation of this one is generating."

Upton points at Gilman and Elwood bookending a petite and dusky woman. "Speaking of strange, aim your headlights at what just walked in. She's two cuts above their usual math groupie."

Dinah: "That's blatant generational prejudice. The lady's majoring in physics, for all you know."

"Mediaeval metaphysics." This from Derby.

Pickman almost sounds impressed: "You know that siren?"

"Only by reputation. Don't you know her?"

"Should I?"

"She's notorious with the university's bohemian set. They're fascinated by her."

"A kindred pariah? Well, Euclid's fourth axiom can't always account for different societal circles. I'm not big on philosophy."

Carter sighs: "You're making my point for me."

Ignoring Carter: "I'm not big on portraits, either, despite my deftness with faces, but something in my Naumkeag blood tells me that temptress would make an apposite subject."

Dinah leans towards Carter. "You feeling all right? You look tired."

Upton leans, too. "Warren working you too hard?"

"'Too hard' again. That *prima donna*. Listen, I'm making ratatouille for dinner. It's one of your favorites. Come home with us after the game and have some. We'd feel better if we knew you were eating."

Pickman: "I like ratatouille, too. I gave you that recipe."

"You also have a trust fund. Couldn't you have at least ordered your best friend some tenders?"

"I offered. You know how proud he is."

Derby: "Do come, Dolph. I've been aching to ask you about the *Necronomicon*."

Carter and Pickman visibly quake as Upton inquires, "The 'what'?"

"*Necronomicon*. It's a grimoire. Perhaps the most infamous. Warren checked out the library's copy." To Carter, "Doctor Armitage was telling me … complaining, actually … about it. Some backwoods geezer from near Dunwich keeps hounding the library wanting to see it."

Pickman to Carter: "Is that why you barred me? Because of some book?"

Derby to Pickman: "I'd appreciate it if I could talk to you about it sometime, too. I've heard your family owns a Greek sixteenth century translation. Miskatonic's copy is a more recent Latin translation."

Carter puts a hand on Pickman's shoulder, unsure he heard right. "*Your* family … the *sangre azul* Pickmans … owns a copy?"

Derby cuts in without meaning: "Why not? After all, one of his ancestors was hanged during the witch trials."

"What the hell?" Pickman brushes away Carter's hand and juts his chin at Derby. "What's wrong with you? Asperger's?"

"It's public record. Cotton Mather watched it."

"That's your excuse for blurting it out? Look, I'm sorry, but I can't say that my family owns any such book."

"But I can." The woman with Gilman and Elwood approaches the table two steps ahead of her chaperons and beams at Derby. "You're well-informed."

Elwood makes introductions: "Hey, Shipwrights, meet Asenath Waite. Asenath, this is The Shipwright Circle."

"You have a club?"

"Just friends minus a coffee house. Derby insists every chic clique needs a name and Algonquin Round Table was taken."

Waite pretends to listen while focusing on Derby, who, Dinah notices, is unable or unwilling to look away.

Gilman jerks a thumb at the nearest TV: "They're about to tipoff."

Carter rises. "The lady can have my chair. I should get back to work."

"But overtime," Pickman reminds him.

"It's above my head. You can have my share of the stir up tonight, if that's all right with Dinah." Carter makes a show of not looking at Pickman as Waite claims his vacated seat.

Elwood: "What's his problem?"

Pickman watches his childhood friend leave. "Nothing good, I'm sure."

5

Randolph Carter tramps home.

Collecting several pages of notes and microcassettes, he unlocks the grimoire and packs the lot into a thirdhand English briefcase. Outside, he treks north up Peabody Avenue before turning west on College Street, where he is startled by a string of explosions from Black Cat firecrackers kicking up slush along the curb on Parsonage Street. Covering his ears, he spots the culprits—some boys scurrying away towards Garrison Street—and for a few unpleasant moments relives the sting of sandy gravel soil sprayed from contraband fireworks that almost lost him his hearing when he was about their age.

Carter makes his way to Northam Williams Hall, one of seven dignified Beaux-Arts buildings on the university's Quadrangle and the seat of the Departments of Psychological and Brain Sciences and of Parapsychology. Heading to the theater-style lecture hall, Carter sits near a rear exit under the balcony, clutching the briefcase in his lap and tapping one foot without realizing it as he waits for Professor Harley Warren to finish with an undergraduate class.

Thirty-five and fit with a penchant for polo shirts and athletic wear, Warren is a bundle of energy behind the podium. "So what should Mankind know? About ourselves? Our world? The cosmos? Even beyond, if possible? Is there knowledge that is beyond our mortal purview to comprehend or accept? If so, how would such knowledge affect a person who stumbles over it or whose curiosity uncovers it? And is it possible that that knowledge might drive one person mad but make another person something beyond a mortal?"

As Carter listens, he observes a man his own age sitting in the front row. Short, trim, blond, and bespectacled with fiercely intelligent blue eyes, the stranger oozes assured impatience, glancing at a wall clock every few minutes while perpetually twitching the dangling foot of a crossed leg.

"Such caveats predate the story of Frankenstein or Proserpine or even Yahweh scolding Job or Adam and Eve. The earliest admonition may appear in the ancient Mesopotamian tale of the sage Adapa, who rejects immortality believing he is actually being offered death. The Mesopotamians associated Adapa with water and believed him to be an advisor to the first king of the city of Eridu, and it's interesting that we find similarities in the Babylonian figure Oannes, who they believed dwelled in the Arabian Gulf from which he would rise each day to bestow wisdom upon Mankind. *Oannes* is also the Greek form of *Uanna*, a name used for Adapa in some Mesopotamian writings. The contemporary writer Berossus describes Oannes as having the body of a fish but underneath that the figure of a man, and this may have led to a popular misbelief—even among scholars—that Adapa-Oannes is identical to the ancient deity Dagon."

Warren breaks off the lecture as class time expires, and Carter wades through the outgoing current of undergrads while watching and straining to hear the blond stranger talking to the professor: "If your lecture topic was for my benefit -- "

"Pure coincidence, Mr. West … unless it benefited you, in which case it was deliberate."

"My decision hasn't changed, if that's what you mean."

Disappointment colors Warren's gaze before he blinks it away. "Of course. I appreciate you coming. If you change your -- "

"I won't."

"I hear you, but at least give some thought to leaving the door open, perhaps as a dual specialty down the road. Allan Halsey tells me you'll make a mean diagnostician or research scientist and he knows his stuff, but so did Hector Muñoz, who was just as convinced you could be an outstanding research or abnormal psychologist. The frontiers of the mind are limitless."

"As are the frontiers of medicine to anyone willing to venture beyond the constricts of tradition."

The left side of Warren's mouth lifts. "That could have been Hector's motto." Warren pauses, as if trying to coax a tell, but the stranger is immobile. "Don't forget, Hector's research was as successful as it was because he was open to other pursuits besides medical science."

"Being a strict proponent of Haeckel, I disagree that Dr. Muñoz's success was anything other than purely medical."

"Haeckel wasn't always right. Recapitulation theory, for instance."

"I fail to see a point. Two centuries before Haeckel there were doctors like Pierre Borel theorizing that a person—dead for centuries—could be resurrected by someone skilled with the proper knowledge and in possession of the decedent's essential salts. Where would we be if championing one or two erroneous theories disqualified an otherwise distinguished body of work? Anyone following his own path has the right to err along the way. Mistakes are part of any path to progress and my path is chosen. I will not be deterred, not even upon the counsel of an admirable peer. Now if you'll excuse me."

Carter waits for West to follow the crowd outside. "I guess he told you."

"Jealous?" Warren scowls. Collects his lecture notes. Frowns. "Sorry. I was trying to do a late colleague a favor. Afraid I failed." Waving an index finger at Carter's briefcase, "What's that?"

"It's for you."

Accepting the case, Warren looks at what is inside. "You finished already?"

"I'm finished with it."

The professor pauses to hear more.

"I'm quit with this book."

"Scares you, does it?"

"It's wearing me down."

"How so?"

"With nightmares."

"Bad dreams? What kind?"

"About End Times and a dark prophet and some otherworldly city hovering off on the horizon."

"Interesting." Warren nods, ponders, and then, "A dream is a dream. That's all it is."

"I take dreams seriously, Harley. Maybe not as much as I once did … but … look, it's not worth it! I just want to sleep again."

Assuming a poker face, Warren takes a front row seat, rests the briefcase on the floor, and steeples his fingertips together. Several seconds later: "I understand."

"So no more research?"

"No more."

"And you'll take my notes?"

"I'll take everything. You're over and done with it."

Softly and slowly: "My job?"

"Carter! You think I'd fire you? Don't you know by now I'm lost without my research assistant? My post-grads usually quit after one semester, but you've put up with me almost three years! Truth is, I applaud you. *Necronomicon* has a reputation for getting under the skin of stronger men than you."

"Thanks. I think."

"Don't be sour. Wise men know their limitations." Then, as if prodded by a notion, "Why don't you get away from Arkham for a few days?"

"You mean take a vacation?"

"A working vacation. That way the school covers your expenses." A palpable wink. "It so happens I'm going to Cutler Bay over spring break. I'm running a profile on the Q.T. for two friends in the Miami-Dade Homicide Bureau. On the way back I want to do a quick survey for Parapsych of a locus that's supposedly weirder then the Coral Castle, and you'd be of invaluable assistance. You can relax in the sun while I loan myself out to Five-O, then help me give the locus an onceover. Who knows? There could be a paper in it." Warren lets this sink in, and then, "What do you say?"

6

"Edward Derby is having impure thoughts."

Derby glances at Waite as he tries to swallow. "What makes you think that? Ratiocination or telepathy?"

"Why not wishful thinking?" The woman stares at Derby as they turn east on High Street to stroll past bare-limbed Norway Maples and the occasional Bradford Pear. "Which do you think it is, young man? The way some people tell it, Asenath Waite is capable of performing all sorts of highly baffling marvels."

"Well, the buzz among the intelligentsia is that she does make them edgy. At least those honest enough to admit it." Inhales. "And I suddenly know how they feel."

"Why 'they'? Don't you consider yourself one of the Miskatonic *Bildungsbürgertum*?"

"I'm no sophisticate."

"Sophisticates are overrated. All their superficially smart language is never going to earn them respect from a scholar like Father or a poet like Justin Geoffrey, and their meaningless ironic prose won't ever equal anything like *Azathoth and Other Horrors*."

"Thank you, but publish or perish isn't just for professors. That collection is nearly the same age as the average freshman, most of who have never heard of it." Derby walks a few more steps. "So your father was Ephraim Waite?"

"You know the answer to that, Edward. You should also know he considers you as much a peer as I'm sure your friend Geoffrey must have."

"Thank you again, but I'm neither's equal."

"Then become one! You have the brain for it. A remarkable man's brain capable of unparalleled accomplishments if seized by the proper knowledge and will."

Derby stops. "How can you be sure of that? We've just met."

"Honestly, Edward, practically your whole life is public knowledge. You entered Miskatonic at age sixteen, majored in English and French literature, and earned high marks in everything except math and science. You've made the university your second home since graduating as well as made yourself invaluable to Dr. Armitage while availing yourself of the library's unrivaled collection of subterranean magical lore. It's also no secret amongst the less risk-adverse students that you've been consorting with the campus purveyors-of-black-magic crowd. Rumor has it you even paid a bit of hush money recently to keep your father from finding out about a ritual that got out of hand in Christchurch Cemetery. If only witches didn't love dancing naked." Blood drains from Derby's face, then gushes back when Waite adds, "I'd have given anything to see that." The woman walks east again, trailing Derby along. "Word also has it you're quite an antiquarian. Architectural history is one of my passions. What can you tell me about … say … a landmark like your club's hangout?"

"We're not a club." Then, as if by rote but trying to impress: "The building is a renovated warehouse. It was commissioned in 1818 by the shareholders of Nicholas Brown and Company after Brown passed away without heirs. Built along Crowninshield Wharf to accommodate the company's expansion from West Indies trading to include the Triangle Trade, the business went into receivership in 1870, after which the warehouse was rented but generally sat neglected. It has survived several hurricanes, most notably the Great Hurricane of 1938, during which the old Island Ferry washed up and all but demolished the boat slip that ran alongside it. The place was on the verge of being condemned when Basil Elton purchased it six years ago and spent the next two years and considerable money renovating it."

"I wonder why he wanted to do that."

"I don't think Basil's ever said why."

Carefully: "Who is Elton?"

"That's a good question. Basil is not his favorite topic of conversation." Still wanting to impress: "He's from Australia … Pilbarra, I think … and quite a maritime historian. He named the tavern after *la Blanche-nef* and he's friends with authorities like St. Julien Perlmutter. That's all I know for sure, but I suspect his family originally came from Cornwall."

"Why's that?"

"Because of a moonrise engraving of a castle he has hanging behind the bar. The castle overlooks the English Channel and you can see some fishing boats and men net fishing, but it's an idyll. Every other portrait or painting in The White Ship is strictly nautical in some way and Basil knows everything about them, but all he claims to know about the engraving is that he found it during the renovation. So I did a little checking and identified it as Trevor Tower near Innsmouth. The artist is William Miller. When I told Basil he didn't seem interested, so I said no more; but, the Trevor family lost their money and lands during the nineteenth century and some parvenu owns the castle now. I can't help wondering if a dispossessed Trevor made his way to Australia."

"Interesting." Waite halts. "What can you tell me about this dwelling?"

Removing his mental blinders to look beyond the woman, Derby recognizes the symmetrical early Georgian Colonial five-bay clapboard with three dormers in its third-storey roof and realizes she has led him into the country. "It's the Crowninshield House."

"Yes?"

"It's one of Arkham's oldest homes. Everybody knows about it."

"What does everybody know?"

"That it was built for Captain John Crowninshield shortly after his family settled in America. The next three generations of Crowninshields lived here before the family joined the ranks of the Boston Brahmins in the 1830s. Arkham has grown westerly away from this locality since then, resulting in the house going unlived in for decades." Eyes the property. "Sad to say that neglect is starting to show."

"I'm purchasing it."

"You're ... ? Pardon?"

"I'm buying it. I'm going to restore it."

"To flip?"

"To reside, but I'll need help." Waite's expression softens to something coquettish. "Wouldn't you live here if you could?"

"I never thought about it ... but it is a wonderful home."

"One that offers isolation yet is very near the university with its library and sophisticates. If you could see this place through my eyes, Edward -- " (something in Waite's voice and expression transfixes Derby as the man dizzies, his legs buckle, and, after a moment that elapses without him, he rebalances to find himself nearer the old house as someone whispers in his ear) " -- you'd want it as much as I do." This new voice sounds like the one Derby hears whenever he updates his voice-mail's greeting. Glancing back, he catches sight of himself, eyes blazing and protruding with an alien mien—then, after another unoccupied moment elapses, he sees Waite staring at him with the same alien mien. Instead of confusion or confoundment, Derby is elated. "It's true! The stories are true!"

"What stories?" Waite teases.

"'Highly baffling marvels.' Such as students insisting you mesmerized them into feeling like you changed personalities with them. I didn't believe them until now! That was amazing!"

Waite closes the distance to brush lips with Derby, not quite kissing him. "Walk me home and tell me how you'd return this house to its former glory."

* * *

7

Walter Gilman finishes his Augustiner.

With an hour to go until last call, Basil Elton refills Gilman's shaker glass. "Sorry about your date."

"Ms. Waite wasn't my date."

"Booty call?"

"In a perfect world." Gilman stares at his beer's bubbles as if searching for rhythm in the tumult. "I'm pretty sure she was only interested in me because of my new apartment."

"Yeah … about that … did ya really pony up what that root rat Elwood said ya did to lay a claim on the most haunted flat in Arkham?"

Gilman levels at the sinewy man in his late fifties with hound dog face, curious hazel eyes of a child, and snow white hair. "I ain't scared of ghosts."

"Who's talking spooks? Mason's a witch. Her familiar's a bloody rat sporting Dwight Frye's head."

"Don't forget their penchant for sacrificing children. *Walpurgisnacht* is just around the corner."

"Don't ya forget that Mason swears she's in cahoots with The Black Man, and ain't nobody had any happy doings with that mongrel." Elton softens. "Listen, what's a basically decent math dag from Haverhill living in a place like that?"

"I don't move in until August."

Elton quietly waits.

"Because I've got this itch. Okay? Renting Mason's room might help me scratch it."

"Okay. So what's got you so stoked?"

Taking a sip, then, "My goal is to be a physicist, and physicists are only as successful as their research. Maxwell had electromagnetism, Bohr the atom, Feynman electrodynamics, and me …? Math is my passion, and I love me some Non-Euclidean and quantum calculus, but their new car smell has faded. String theory is kind of sexy, but too many researchers are already spelunking that rabbit hole, which, I.M.H.O., has too many little doors and not enough 'Drink Me' bottles."

"Fair enough. Ya figure on backtracking to see if any Albertus Magnus or Raymond Lully types might have something to teach ya, Dr. Frankenstein."

"I wouldn't have put it that way. I'm focusing on folklore, not alchemy."

"What sorta folklore?"

"Sorcery-legend. I never paid attention to such stories before moving here, but this city's lousy with them. You can't swing a slipstick without knocking one over, and after awhile it all permeates your brain. And don't get me started with the Puritan trials! Banaczek's house is far from the only one where a witch hid from the King's men during the days of Province."

"Granted, but it is the best known one. Plus that Shelia's one of the few witches to give the slip to Arkham's Gaol."

"Yes, and it's how she supposedly got away that fascinates me. First she bragged at her trial that she could use lines and curves during Witches' Sabbaths to point out directions beyond the walls of space to other spaces. Then she left behind lines and angles she allegedly drew with something like blood on the walls of her empty cell which even Cotton Mather couldn't decipher. Now, if any of that's true, where the hell did some old woman in the seventeenth century acquire that kind of mathematical insight? It's stories like hers that give me the itch to research connections between mathematics and legends of elder magic; and I've got to tell you, the atmosphere in Mason's room … when I stepped into it this afternoon … it's stimulating! For one thing, its lines of perspective are off. They're just off! Who'd even want to build a room like that?"

"Dr. Caligari maybe."

"Make jokes if you want, Basil, but I need to find out." A thought. "Maybe I should ask Pickman to check out Mason's room sometime. Artists are all about perspective. Zero-point … one-point … two-point … etcetera. He might have some observations or opinions. You know, there are rare grimoires like the *Necronomicon* that supposedly record abstract formulae on the properties of space and the linkage of known and unknown dimensions, and Derby says Pickman's family owns a copy."

"I thought the drongo told ya Derby was wrong."

"He did, but I got the feeling Pickman doth protest too much. Even Carter acted like he didn't believe R.U. Not that it matters. If need be, nobody has a better collection of grimoires than my future alma mater's library."

Elton crosses his arms to think. "Let's say you're right. What's your end-game? What's your pot of gold?"

"I think I'm half Jewish so I'll answer your question with a question. What if Mason didn't escape her cell by squeezing through the bars or bribing the jailer or apparition or twitching her nose? What if she deliberately stepped from the earth to a mathematically juxtaposed body or zone of space?"

"Ya mean a wormhole? Ain't places like MIT and Stanford studying them?"

"Yes, Einstein-Rosen bridges are connected with mass analysis of electromagnetic field energy; however, my research is the background of multi-dimensional reality in folklore, which, as far as I can tell, nobody else is even considering. It's virgin territory."

Elton let his expression speak for him.

"Look, I know my notion that there's something mathematically … scratch that … cosmically relevant inherent in folklore sounds like a *National Enquirer* headline, but I've just got to pursue it. Since I'll only be wasting my time and money if my theory turns out to be *bupkis*, what harm is there checking it out?"

8

"Harley Warren is ready to rock!"

Carter remembers tugging his scarf tighter around his neck as Warren said this.

"What's wrong, Grasshopper? You haven't said a word since we turned off 41."

"When have I had the chance? You've been crowing non-stop about unearthing 'something wonderful' while helping the police since we left Cutler Bay."

"None of which you heard from me. I signed a non-disclosure agreement."

"Your transgression is safe, so long as you turn up the heat."

Warren only chuckled. "After this winter, you're lucky I don't roll down the windows or turn on the AC. It's almost sixty."

The dashboard thermometer registered almost fifty and didn't take into account Florida's terminal humidity. "Why not wait to do this survey tomorrow like you'd planned? We'll have daylight and it'll be warmer."

"Too warm. I'm doing you a favor."

"You think so? I'm not as warm-blooded as you."

"Well, you prefer working at night."

"I do. At home."

"Well, some things can only be done after sunset, and this job's turned into one."

Carter had no doubts inquiring why would only prompt another homily, and, since they were not turning back, he could use a few moments repose. Ever since Warren left the Gainesville Pike for the backroad taking them into Big Cypress Swamp it had felt like they were travelling down a burrow through the dense forest, the skeletal limbs of flanking wet cypress trees clutching overhead. The last thing Carter could recall for sure about the drive later was counting boughs to try to forget about the chill and a gnawing claustrophobia; then, he realized, Warren was shaking him.

"We're here. Grab some gear. Each of us carries a bag."

"We're 'where'?"

"Where do you think?" Warren climbed out of the crossover. "Come on."

"Half a sec." Discomfited they had parked without it registering, Carter was delighted to have dozed off for the first time in weeks without suffering any End Times dreams. So delighted that he paid scant attention to his next few actions and assumed he must have exited the CUV, collected one of two weighty Filson duffels that had jangled like plumber bags during the drive, and trailed after Warren into the woods.

Carter distinctly recollected stink and moonlight as they entered an oval hollow surrounded by a ring of trees—tall as giants—that blotted everything except a waning crescent in a hazy sky. Foul vapors seeped from cancerous growths of grass, moss, and weeds that mixed with the reek of putrefying stone from a glut of urns, slabs, mausoleum facades, and cenotaphs—many of peculiar design—being consumed by insatiable eons and verdure. Any stones whose carvings had not been scoured by the years and elements featured ideograms that were unfamiliar to Carter, several of which resembled marine life and objects.

"I'll ask again: where are we?" He found himself sweating in spite of the chilly air. "The locus. We've strayed off the beaten path, haven't we?" Warren dropped his duffel and pulled out an LED flashlight to read a codex no bigger than a mass-market paperback. The cover's sable hide was devoid of markings, and, when Warren opened the book, Carter failed to recognize its pictographic writing, which incorporated many of the ideograms and curvilinear mathematical designs from the stones.

"What's that writing? Naacal?"

Warren smiled.

"Harley, what's that book?"

"Something wonderful."

Carter shivered. "That's what you uncovered?"

"Yes. An unusual Yogi collected this … along with certain other things … during his travels. It was lost after making its way from France to New England, and I had an inkling my subjects might have laid their hands on this without fully understanding what they possessed. Good thing, too." Pause. "We never could have located this place without it."

"So what is it? A map? Guide book?"

"It's a grimoire."

Carter rattled. "Not *Al Azif?*"

"Does it look like a *Necronomicon?*" Warren chuckled. Flipped a page. "It's more like an apocrypha."

"Damn it! You agreed -- !"

"Will you forget about *Al Azif* and concentrate on the job? This necropolis is without precedent in any scholarly annals. We're treading in pristine territory here!"

Carter felt on the verge of loathing any form of the word *precedent* as he asked, "Just how pristine?"

"Whatever do you mean?"

"Is this a protected area? Is that why we have to do this at night? Are you doing this survey for Parapsych on the Q.T., too?"

"I was speaking academically and I'm the only member of the department who knows about this locus. I'd also like to keep it that way until I submit our survey." Before Carter could fulminate: "I know this was a dirty trick, but consider the circumstances. An opportunity like this is extraordinary! We may never get a chance like this again in our careers." That said: "Now, best as I can verify, this necropolis is reserved for worshippers of an exceptionally nasty cult, but the place is so old they must have lost track of it. It predates De Leon, Henry the Navigator's explorers, the Tequesta … Christ, even the alligator, if you can believe that."

"Let's say I don't, there are hundreds of scholarly annals about secret religions."

"Not about this bunch. They guard their secrets. The past, however, will divulge even the song the Sirens sang or Achilles's name among Lycomedes's daughters to the right person if it takes the notion." Warren patted the codex against his breast before tucking it into a back pocket of his cargo pants, grabbed a duffel, and motioned Carter to bring up the rear as he searched among the tombs with the flashlight. "The apocrypha claims that corpses resting here never decay, but lay firm and fat, as if sleeping, as they wait for the stars to be right again."

Carter nearly bolted. "What do you mean by that?"

"Not sure." Warren never stopped searching. "It doesn't go into details."

"That's what Nyarlathotep says."

Lured by something more interesting in his beam, Warren dropped to a knee in front of a half-obliterated sepulcher, and, almost as an after-thought, asked, "The dark prophet from your nightmares?"

"That's him."

"Descendent of Azathoth, right?"

"As well as the messenger of the Great Old Ones, which includes the high priest Cthulhu, who lies dead and dreaming until 'the stars are right.'"

"And then what? Your apocalypse kicks off."

"Yes! I don't think we should be here!"

"Why? For Heaven's sake, you think the stars happen to be right tonight? Even if they are, can we do anything about it?"

"No … not really."

"Then let's eat, drink, and survey." Warren paced as he made a series of mental measurements in relation to the sepulcher, halted in front of a mound, then pulled a folding spade from his duffel and instructed Carter to do the same. "Remember, Grasshopper, nothing in the world is worth having without pain, effort, difficulty." The men spent several minutes digging until they had exhumed three immense granite slabs. Even without the flashlights Carter could see the surfaces had been preserved by the moss-grown earth that had washed over the blocks over innumerable years. Warren remarked, "As bare as the codex's cover."

"You knew these were under here?"

Instead of answering, Warren jammed the edge of his spade under the slab nearest the sepulcher and pried.

"Harley, wait! Let's take pictures! Make a record -- !"

"Moonlight's wasting!" Kept trying. "It's … really … stuck! Give me a hand, Sisyphus!"

Carter obeyed.

The men strained until a seal of muck and roots gluing down the granite cracked. Tipping the slab to one side, they were awashed by a corrupt stench that escaped the earth like evils from Pandora's Box.

"Getbackgetback!"

Gagging and rubbing eyes, the men waited for the miasma to slacken before Warren pointed his flashlight into the cut.

"Where are the corpses?" Carter asked.

The beam exposed a flight of damp stone steps and moist walls encrusted with niter that descended beyond the ray's reach.

A whispered moan from Warren: "So it's true."

"You knew about these, too? Harley, what's going on?"

"Nothing we can't handle."

Warren brought his duffel beside the cut and unpacked. First a white metal storage case that reminded Carter of a vanity suitcase, then a bundle of copper-colored rods, and lastly two lightweight cables. "You've got this stuff in your bag, but leave it in there. You need the flashlight, though." As Carter rummaged for the flashlight, Warren shoved six of the rods into the earth on either side of the storage case, connected each half-dozen to one cable, then spliced both cables into one plug. Next he detached the case's lid, inserted the plug into a jack marked ANTENNA in the upper left corner of a control panel, and depressed an ON/OFF button dummy-protected by two semi-circle metal posts in the panel's lower left corner. Instantly an LED touchscreen control in the panel's center illumed. "This is the surface unit. Your bag has the subsurface unit. These beauties put a dent in my 401K, but they're going to be worth it."

"What are they?"

"The finest TTE communication technology civilians can own. Uses bidirectional text messaging capable of transmitting up to fifteen hundred meters through the earth. I hope I don't have to go that far, but it's nice to know my limits."

Carter gawked at the cut as a fleeting spark of admiration was engulfed by panicked comprehension. "No!"

"We have to find out where the corpses are."

"You can't go down there! Not alone!"

"And share the discovery?" Warren smirked. "It's only a hole. The surface unit will display my texts, but I need you to record them. There's a logbook and pens in my duffel."

Carter made himself ask, "What are you going to report on down there?"

A broader, richer smirk. "Nothing you can imagine. Certainly nothing a bundle of nerves like you ought to see. Not if you couldn't finish --"

"Will you forget about *Al Azif?*"

"Was that an echo?" Warren winks. "Don't fret. I'm the professor. The responsibility is all mine."

"That's not why I'm worried! Listen, if you take one step towards those stairs, I swear I'll leave! If I have to walk back to Cutler Bay … to Arkham … I will!"

"Which gets you what? Besides blisters? I can always come back with someone else. Not a grad assistant; you're without peer; but I bet Dr. Burke would jump at a chance like this after missing the cut on the latest Antarctic expedition." Warren traded his smirk for a look of sincerity. "Not that I could find anyone better than Randolph Carter to be my Michael Collins. I need you. What do you say?"

Carter wanted to argue but succumbed to adulation. "Fine."

"There you go!" Warren slipped the strap of Carter's duffel over his shoulder, stepped into the cut, then smiled. "'That's one small step for Man,' eh? Listen, I'll show you how much I appreciate your loyalty later, but, for right now, don't get any notions about butting in. It won't do you any good so long as I possess the real key to this affair." Warren tapped the codex with one hand then started downward again.

Carter watched Warren's beam dwindle and listened to the sharp, decisive blows of his boots recede. Eventually the ray vanished, as if Warren had turned a corner, and the stairwell went still, but Carter kept watching. When the light did not reappear, he dumped the remaining contents out of Warren's duffel, patted the bag flat, sat, grabbed the logbook and pen, and commenced to wait.

Alone.

Alone with the incessant moonlight, humid night chill, and muffled, almost distant hullabaloo of frogs, owls, and crickets.

Alone yet bound to the unknown depths by more than the TTE.

Carter worshipped Warren.

What other reason was there for him tolerating the monster? And Carter had no delusions that Warren was one of Joseph Campbell's fear-haunted, self-independent tyrant-monsters who confuse the havoc wrecked by their impulsive egos as humane intentions.

Carter also feared Warren.

After spending four years as an undergrad studying under Warren and three years as the man's assistant, Carter feared he was willingly being absorbed by a personality who embodied … epitomized … everything he had desired to be since childhood. Warren was erudite and imaginative, authoritative and charming, respected by intelligentsia and admired by common folk, and tolerant yet indefatigably indomitable. If this situation was permitted to continue, Carter feared that he would grow incapable of refusing his paragon anything, which would explain why he went on waiting alone when the commonsensical thing to do was to ditch Warren without ever looking back.

Randolph Carter was a researcher, not a psychologist or parapsychologist, and, despite his dabblings in myths, legends, folklore, and religion, he possessed a chronic impatience with any feeble member of humanity afflicted with the cancer of superstition. The same could be said for Warren, whose interest in parapsychology was an extension of his work as a criminal profiler. Warren understood that the best criminal psychiatrists comprehended irruptions of the irrational as violations of intelligence; that the best parapsychologists appreciated them as the contravention of aesthetic norms; and that the best profilers applied both absolutes to get a leg up on their subjects. The best profiler comprehended that the unintelligible was necessarily hideous but appreciated that it often obeyed laws of artistic creation discernible in mythical abstractions like theogonies, liturgies, and ritual as well as wanton play and diversion. Rather than dismiss a grimoire like *Al Azif* as "the daughter of disbelief" like Louis Vax or as dogma with an obsession on infamy and sacrilege, Warren researched it hoping to glean insights into the inverted aesthetic of the systemization of transgression.

At least, that's how Warren explained it whenever he was asked on *Book TV*.

Fearful as Carter was of turning into some kind of Trilby or William Wilson, he was suddenly more worried about the cult responsible for the necropolis.

They guard their secrets.

Maybe they hadn't forgotten about the cemetery.

Maybe they kept watchmen here.

Warren and Carter were not only trespassers, they had despoiled a grave.

How would the cult react, rather it caught them *in flagrante delicto* or learned of the violation later? Warren mentioned collaborating on a paper!

More worrisome still was the stone steps.

Where did they lead? If they predated the Tequesta and the alligator, who had excavated them? And what had induced someone to cover them with the slab?

There are no atheists in foxholes, and, when it came to the vertical axis of the imagination, Carter could not think of anything good to be found in the entrails of the earth; so, while his skepticism in the numinous was total and definitive, at this hour, as he waited amongst whatever swamp dryads and mould ghouls called the forsaken deadland home, Carter envisioned something awful and primordial waiting in the timeless depths below for release.

Telegraphic lights flickered from the TTE's touchscreen.

Carter lunged over the control panel, holding his breath.

U getting this?

Carter suspired, cautiously relieved. U OK?

Yep. Worried? :)

Been 15 minutes.

Slickery stairs. Hot here 2. Ud like it.

:-p

Carter made a note in the logbook of the hour and minute displayed in the touchscreen's upper right corner in military time.

Warren's next text did not arrive for nearly a minute: Eureka! Half a sec!

A heaping expectation and a spoonful of vexation supplanted Carter's midnight fears. Surely any cult that abandoned so imposing a cemetery must be extinct, which would explain how Warren could not only get his hands on the apocrypha but lead them here without repercussion. Instead, Carter's mentor was about to reveal a momentous discovery in pagan … .

Lights flickered again.

Carter read: AWAKE! PUT SLAB BCK! ITS CMING!

What?

BEATITBETITBEAT

An echo of what might have been a faraway scream wafted from the cut.

Carter scurried down the stairs.

Three steps down the ground quaked as if punched by a giant hand beneath the earth and knocked him off his feet.

He landed hard.

Buckled his ribs.

Puked air from his lungs.

Suddenly his body did not want to work right.

Dropped the flashlight.

Carter willed himself to breathe between clenched teeth as his flashlight tumbled like a runaway keg until it smacked against the place where Warren's beam had vanished. There it laid, rocking a bit, ray shining a foot or two before terminating at a wall or passageway.

For several seconds there was no noise except the constant ringing in his ears.

Carter struggled to get vertical. Head spinning. Body throbbing. Lungs reengaging. Then he felt as much as heard the percussion of what sounded like enormous footfalls.

Something large was coming.

"Harley?" Carter wheezed.

No reply.

A little louder but no firmer: "Harley?"

Still no reply as the footfalls stopped and something eclipsed the ray as it billowed up the steps. A gale with the wail of a horrendous chorus of cicadas followed, herding Carter outside. He grappled to try to slide the slab over the cut until his ribs and whatever was coming compelled him to break for the nearest tree line.

Crippled by injury, unable to think about anything except Abdul Alhazred in Samarra, Carter expected every hobble to be his last. Like Alhazred, Carter refused to turn his head, at least until he reached the cypresses, where he bounced off boles and slewed to a stop. Paralyzed by pain, exhausted, and praying the trees veiled him, Carter watched a ceaseless tenebrous shadow spew from the cut to drape the moonlight. When the gale breached its wail metamorphosed into a flute-like twittering that called age-old thought memories and stirred dim primal deeps lurking inside Carter's brain. The apocalypse from his nightmares bloomed before Carter's mind's eye, but, instead of civilization's conditioned revulsion and horror, a dormant desire for carnage and revelry was reawakened. Simultaneously three red glimmers blossomed within the shadow, their bourgeoning luminosity silhouetting some of the caliginous folds collecting into a colossal amorphous body. Other folds gathered into more definite forms: a pair of titan wings and six immense spiny legs that tapered to a single strong claw. The legs spread to buttress themselves into the ground between tombs as the lights synchronized, gyrated, and crystallized into a sparkling blood-teared three-lobbed eye. Then, as Carter buried his face in the dirt, the chthonic being's wings flapped to take flight.

* * *

9

Randolph Carter is losing his mind.

How else can he explain having no memory of making his way to County Road 94? Yet that is where he was discovered wandering that morning, bleached as a bone, by a pair of gypsy truck drivers. Carter also does not recall being admitted to a trauma room at NCH Baker Hospital in Naples. The first thing he can recollect is giving his statement to Warren's sensible middle-aged friends, Lieutenants Hart Crane and Sam Loveman, concluding at the point where he fell in the tomb.

"I'm not sure what happened after that."

Crane and Loveman appeared worried about Warren, but Carter sensed they were even more concerned about how the profiler acquired the apocrypha. The detectives were in a better mood when they visited Carter a second time to inform him they could not locate the cemetery or the backroad, but did find Warren.

"Harley's all right?"

"Fit as the proverbial fiddle," Loveman said. "He's in his hotel room."

"Then he told you -- "

Crane: "Harley's been there since last night. He says he doesn't know about your book or cemetery."

Carter waggled his head as his heart sunk. "He -- "

"He says he came back to the hotel and you were gone. No note or explanation." Slightly softer: "He also mentioned you've been stressing a little lately. An unusual workload."

Loveman came in, as if on cue: "You've got to admit ... that statement of yours ... hey ... stress can knock anyone out of whack. We've been there."

"Yes, but -- " Carter started.

"You have no marks on your body. Your tox screen came back negative, thank God, what with the mickeys getting slipped these days. An attack of the nerves, though, would explain how you ended up like a zombie on the Loop Road."

"Unless Warren is lying."

Loveman nodded as Crane asked, "There's that. But why?"

To cover his arse, Carter did not say out loud.

Crane continued, "We ain't saying you didn't have something happen to you last night, but can't you remember anything besides that graveyard stuff?"

Carter appreciated the diplomacy, and—truth be told—he had begun to wonder if all the wild special effects that occurred after Warren went spelunking had not been conjurations of his fall, the morbid environment, his delving into the *Al Azif* plus his nightmares. It was even possible Carter could have imagined Warren's scream, although it and Warren's frantic texts were in character with the man's sardonic sense of humor, just as Harley's intolerable lie was in character for a tyrant-monster. Carter therefore decided that the most prudent thing for himself and Warren was to say he remembered nothing else but also nothing more.

The detectives left in due course, and, eventually, a trauma specialist suggested that Carter remain overnight. "For observation." Carter acquiesced, but, except for assuring the admin assistant there was no immediate next-of-kin to contact, he paid scant attention to anything until he was wheeled into his own room. There he fixed his eyes on the ceiling and did his best to squirrel away the previous eighteen or so hours into a compartment of his brain.

Sooner or later Carter drifted asleep.

Sometime after sunset a nurse appeared.

Carter noticed an untouched dinner plate on the adjustable table beside his bed and assumed the ashen young woman with murky eyes, clipped raven hair, and Tyrian red scrubs was fetching it, but, instead, she announced, "You have a visitor."

Without thinking: "The police again?"

"Harley Warren."

Carter kept still.

"He was worried."

Carter kept on keeping still.

"Send him in?"

Afraid he would forgive Warren if the monster gained admittance: "Please tell Dr. Warren I'm sleeping."

"He -- "

"Please."

Carter shut his eyes as if returning to sleep.

When he dared to peek, the nurse was gone.

In her stead was the TTE surface unit.

Carter gawked and sighed. "What were Doc Holliday's last words?" Nevertheless, he brought the unit back to Arkham with him, along with Florida's tropical weather.

At least twice a day for six unseasonably hot and humid days Carter picked up his phone to call the university's messenger service to have them deliver the unit to Warren, but never followed through. Carter would have liked to think that Warren left the unit as a symbolic gesture that he would be ready to communicate if Carter felt up to it. More likely, though, it was a sophomoric ploy to coax Carter into seeing him under the obligation of returning the unit. Carter had no doubts that he himself had done the commonsense thing in the swamp—unintentional as it was—and that returning the unit by messenger service was just as commonsensical since it would 1) confirm that Warren should find a new research assistant, and 2) hopefully, put an end to Carter's fears. Nevertheless, Carter brought the unit to Northam Williams Hall late in the afternoon of the seventh day.

Thunder from a nascent spring storm rumbled and the steam whistle at the university's power plant wailed as Carter arrived at Warren's office.

"Five o'clock already?" Warren smiled as he accepted the unit. "What do you say to some dinner? You like the French onion soup at Joseph's, don't you? You speak French, so that makes perfect sense. It's my treat, of course. I feel I owe you something."

To be fair, that was more of an apology then Carter expected. "Thanks, but no."

"Oh?"

"I just want to return your property."

"I see." Warren let some time pass before adding, "I appreciate that."

"You're welcome." Carter swallowed. He needed to ask: "What happened?"

Warren fiddled with the unit's latch. "'Happened'?"

"'Cut it out. I thought you were in trouble."

"'Trouble'?"

In a rush: "I heard you scream! I read your texts!" Carter took a breath. "If you were pulling my leg, so be it, but at least tell me if you found whatever it was you were searching for. You owe me that much."

Warren seemed to be giving this serious consideration when he fiddled too hard, the latch opened, the lid separated, and the unit tumbled to the floor as the storm erupted outside.

Without thinking Carter went on his knees to retrieve the unit, but when he looked up Warren was gone and in his stead stood Nyarlathotep. Swarthy, slender, and sinister with the bearing of a pharaoh, Nyarlathotep pointed at the unit.

Writ upon the control panel: HARLEY WARREN IS DEAD.

Carter, staggered, mind blasted, laughed.

He is still laughing when campus police arrive several minutes later to find him alone, without the unit, in the office.

"I don't like this, boss."

CHAPTER TWO

VAGUE GHOSTS OF MONSTROUS THINGS

1

Harris House stands silent and alone.

The spring storm has spewed over Providence, Rhode Island. Cool winds overwhelmed the balmy diurnal air, thunder and lightning continue to burst about the churning clouds like the Blitz, and rain peppers the ambered Colonial lanes of College Hill, where, hunkered on the east side of Benefit Street, is Harris House.

A narrow semi-farm building with an unusually peaked roof and blackish unpainted exterior, it is inset in a steep lawn and embowered by contorted ash and elms shunned by birds and insects. Cockeyed mossy steps cut through the grayish grass and malformed weeds along its west wall, leading towards the second and third stories and dormerless attic. A deep cellar exposed by years of road widening provides southern street frontage with a door and two windows.

Harris House has a reputation.

Tainted by an unnatural frequency of calamities, no one has lived here in decades, yet, on many a night, a sickly yellow corpse-light has been seen flickering through the cellar windows. Tonight, however, Harris House is not empty, and, as the yellow light flickers, someone screams.

The cellar door opens.

Within a gurgling like a bubbling cauldron crescendos in conjunction with an incoherent chorus of Gallic and English moans.

A young man flees the cellar, smearing greasy green footsteps on the sidewalk in his wake.

A trickle of the same fetid ichor seems to follow him outside.

The downpour washes away both footsteps and trickle.

Inside the cellar the cacophony and corpse-light die and Harris House stands silent and alone once more.

2

"Randolph Carter is receiving many visitors."

Not that they come all at once. The drive from Arkham to the Massachusetts Hospital School in Canton takes more than an hour, so The Shipwright Circle individually pay their respects as schedules permit, each one getting a brief orientation beforehand from Harold Barnard, the abnormal psychiatrist assigned to Carter's case since the patient's release from the crisis stabilization ward.

"Visitors are good, but remember Randolph is suffering from a catatonic stupor, so don't be intimidated or discouraged if he fails to react to you. Depression can make executing even simple things extremely difficult if not impossible."

Dinah is the first caller. After presenting Barnard with some clothes and necessities for the patient in a black carry-on suitcase she scrounged from one of Carter's closets, she peppers the doctor with questions about Carter's NMDA prescription and repetitive transcranial magnetic stimulation treatments as he escorts her to the patient's room in the open unit. Dinah presents Carter with a homemade Get Well Soon card cobbled from black and orange construction paper and signed by the Uptons and Derby. "Eddie's underage or he'd be here, but he said to be sure to tell you, 'Howahyah?' Daniel plans to visit this weekend, but with that deadline for the university's new administration building coming up, it might be next week. Edward promises to visit soon, but, to be honest, even we don't see him much lately." Dinah waits out of habit, but when Carter does not reply: "It's Asenath Waite. They spend more time together every day." Dinah waits again before continuing, and, unencumbered by replies, unburdens her mind. "I love Edward. You know I do. You've said it yourself, though. He behaves more like a freshman than a middle-aged man. It hasn't helped he's so shy around strangers and doesn't have the greatest self-esteem. Classic writer syndrome compounded by his mother coddling him till the day she died. Did you know he's never had a girlfriend? So maybe an adult relationship might ripen him, even if it's with a flapper. Eddie misses him, though. So does Daniel." Pause. "My hubby won't say anything, but I can tell he's worried, and I don't blame him. Waite has a roving eye. I've caught her ogling me and other women quite a few times. The way she does it ... like some dirty old man ... it's creepy. Quite frankly, Waite's just weird, which is hardly a campus secret."

Pickman visits later, bringing a Blick Art Materials sack with him and looking atypically intimidated and chagrined. Feigning a Cagney impersonation: "Who'd have thunk you'd have anything to do with this place again? I got an idea to bust you out, though, pal. Hit me on the way here." Removing a Strathmore heavyweight drawing pad and a set of paper-wrapped charcoal pencils from the sack: "Knowing how you loathe having your picture taken, I figure me drawing your caricature should get you chirping in no time." Pickman begins. Speaking in his regular voice: "I hear you, I hear you. 'Very subtle, R.U.' Well, *le chevalier*, we don't have time for subtle. Life's too short and this place too full of memories. Not just your folks but you almost ending up here, too." Looks up. "Now that I think about it, you always cut me off whenever I try to apologize for that. So just say something if you want me to stop." Clears his throat. "You were right that day. You and I and the rest of the Slater Avenue Army had no business playing with Tanner's cherry bombs. I also know Coleman shouldn't have just dropped that one he couldn't get lit, just like I know I shouldn't have picked it up and flung it away without looking after its fuse sparked." Turns somber. "I thought I was being brave. I swear I didn't know that you were behind me." Shakes his head. "And then ... when you couldn't get rid of that ringing in your ears ... and it almost drove you ... well ... I would have cut my hand off if it would have brought you relief." There is no response from Carter. "Sometimes it seems the only thing I do right is the wrong thing." Pickman goes back to sketching until it becomes apparent it is serving as a bromide for him rather than a curative for Carter. "Okay, since we're making a clean breast of things here, Derby was right when he said we Pickmans own a copy of the *Necronomicon*." Silence. "I suppose it's what you'd call an heirloom from that ancestor who died of Hempen fever, although I could stretch Derby's neck for blurting that out, public record be damned. And it's not like I was the only one at that table with a forefather brought before the Court of Oyer and Terminer." Deep breath in, out, and counts to three. "I'm sorry. That was uncalled for … but, before Derby interrupted, I was getting ready to tell you that your idol, Harley Warren, had inquired about purchasing our copy earlier that day. He got the same muddle as Derby. Look, I'm sorry I obfuscated, but neither of those Peter Pans has any business mixing it up with that book. *Er lasst sich nicht lessen.* Not without consequences. Then I started thinking, if Warren couldn't buy our copy, how long would it be before he had you annotating the MU library's copy, if you weren't already? I was worried one of you might uncover things below you shouldn't know about." Pickman rubs his right eye with the back of his drawing hand. "Maybe that's why you're here." Rubs his left. Droops his head. "I hope not." Blinks. Grimaces. "And why on earth did they admit you here? Even Arkham Sanitarium would have been better. Don't they know better?"

Gilman comes next, as excited as a kid on Christmas Eve about his impending change of address. "I've even been dreaming about Mason's room. Really vivid ones where I see every asymmetry and can hear a clock or death watch ticking." Worry corrugates his brow. "That isn't weird? Is it? Elwood thinks I'm bound for the room next to yours … sorry, he's not always the most tactful … but couldn't it just be my imagination blowing off steam? If the mind doesn't vent, it'll explode. That just makes sense." Eager again. "And I can't stop thinking about moving from academic to action research. Yes, I've got plenty of prep work to keep me busy this summer. And, yes, smart men study physics and von Juntz, but wise men do it in small doses. I've just got this itch. I sense … something … going on. Something apart from the clockworks of the universe. It's science and myth pooled or maybe beyond that. I mean, how much of creation is jumbled? How much is connected? How much is whole? How much of it is benevolent? Ambivalent? Malevolent? That sounds a little like Edward Jessup, maybe, but I bet Mason sensed it, too. I bet she also discovered at least some answers, because she grasped how to use mathematics too advanced for her contemporaries, or became a math adept in the learning. Imagine that! Being so far afield from any other human. So isolated. Think about how Sidis suffered, and he wasn't living with Puritans."

When Derby arrives he is a few pounds trimmer and sporting his most recent stab at cultivating a mustache. "I suppose Dinah told you about Asenath." Derby grins. "Everyone insists we're a couple, even the ABD erudites, but they're easily impressed with surface aspects. Not that I'd mind if we were, but, whatever kind of unit we are, we're definitely platonic … though she talks very daring at times." Wiggles his eyebrows. "I can honestly say that Asenath has her detractors, her fans, even a couple wannabe hanger-ons, but I'm her lone friend outside of Innsmouth." Mirth fades. He starts to say, "About that … her being from Innsmouth … " On second thought: "I've never met anyone as adept in eldritch lore. She knows things other people don't, which shouldn't be surprising. I know you know about her father, Ephraim Waite, and Asenath likes to say she's his best pupil."

Daniel Upton spends part of his visit likewise assessing Derby and Waite's relationship. "They're feelings for each other are intimate. That's apparent whenever she looks at him and vice versa. It's just that I'd classify Edward's feelings as adoration.

He admires the woman. On the other hand, Waite's feelings are possessive." Deliberates that. "No. That's not quite right. Waite clearly admires Edward, but the way she looks at him is predatory. Viewed in hindsight, I suppose their feelings reflect their personalities. In any case, woe unto him that tries untangling that pair." More deliberating. "I'm sharing a confidence, but Edward's father stopped by my office after hours the other night. He told me that he pressed Edward about Waite and Edward confessed that he expects to marry her. I have no idea how she feels, but I do have it on good authority that she's making inroads towards purchasing the Crowninshield House; which, rather intentional or not, only makes her more attractive to him." Almost blushing: "I'm not proud of this, but, ever since I found that out, I've been tempted to volunteer my services to assist her with restoring that landmark." Coy grin. "Anyway, Mr. Derby asked if I might talk to Edward to try to change his mind. 'Because of her reputation and bloodline, you understand.' He meant well, even if he kept referring to Edward as 'the boy,' which, if you ask me, is part of the problem. Edward is immature in many ways because of how his parents raised him. That's not his fault, but I'm afraid it's resulted in his transferring dependence from his parent to a mate. I suppose that was inevitable, unless Edward became a recluse."

Later that evening, Barnard is walking out when a newscast on the common room television catches his attention and he halts beside Carter. According to the newsreader, the Providence police are asking for the public's assistance in their search for physician and local historian Elihu Whipple, who was last seen leaving his home on North Court Street several days earlier. Barnard shakes his weary head and murmurs, "Where are you, Eli?"

"You two are friends?"

Barnard glances at Carter, who remains unresponsive in his wheelchair, then turns towards the only other patient in the common room, who peaks up from a ratty hardcover. "Good friends. Yes."

"For a long time?"

"We were undergrads together." Barnard identifies the young man as Lawrence Olmstead, diagnosed with somatic delusion and comorbid biological degeneration with osseous factors associated with a hereditary condition regionally referred to as the Innsmouth look. "Was it you who upset Mr. Carter's visitor the other day, Lawrence?"

"Edward Derby? I enjoy his poetry."

"Of course, but please check with an attendant before approaching visitors."

Olmstead stares, never blinking.

"What's that you're reading?"

"*In Search of the Unknown.*"

"Don't think I've heard of it. From our library?"

"By Robert W. Chambers. And, no."

"I like the title. I might look it up on AbeBooks." Barnard glances at the television. The newscast has progressed to the weather. "Good night, Lawrence." Pats Carter's shoulder. "Good night, Randolph. Don't stay up too late, boys."

Carter says nothing.

Barnard returns to his book.

* * *

3

Randolph Carter's nightmare returns.

This time it commences in Northam Williams Hall. Carter is sitting under the balcony near the rear exit of the lecture hall, his English briefcase between his legs, as he waits for Warren to finish with an undergraduate class.

Warren is gripping the apocrypha. "So what should Mankind know?" Pats its cover. "There are certain dark and dusty and half-lost books of crumbling elder lore with words that keep monstrous secrets." Sweeps a hand to implicate the audience. "Secrets that may drive you to nighted worlds of ill or …" Stops at Carter. "… to the throne of some high home of ray-streamed domes and towers."

Carter observes West in the front row, oblivious to a portly, disheveled intellectual of sixty sitting immediately behind him and glaring at the doctor. Also in the audience are Crane and Loveman—the detectives cheerfully complaisant as they watch Warren brandish the apocrypha—and Gilman—insipid and spent. Something the size of a large brown kitten is curled in Gilman's lap, its head and feet tucked out of sight. Carter glances back West's way and the intellectual has been supplanted by a distinguished, natty, and vigorous middle-aged gentleman who could pass for his frumpy predecessor's younger brother. A bipedal creature with rubbery skin and a face resembling a canine as much as Pickman slumps into the seat beside Carter to glibber a ghoulish word in his ear, wink, and instruct, "Remember that for *auld lang syne*." Meanwhile, Warren begins to transform like wafting smoke to the accompaniment of flapping elephantine wings and a high, thin whining from the balcony. Waxing taller and thinner, skin dimming dusky, clothes flowing into sunset red raiment, and eyes sparkling bold and dark, a bowed hush falls over the hall as the people await the spiel of Nyarlathotep.

"Such secrets predate Mankind. They were molded into the depths of the dreams of the first men by the Great Old Ones, they who exist outside Time and Space. When the stars are right, the Great Old Ones plunge to worlds like this one, which they rule with chaos. Now they wait, dead yet sleeping by the spells of the priest Cthulhu, for the stars to be right once again. They wait while their cults of nocturnal worshippers fan their flames in dark woods and lonely places until the day they are revived and reignite a holocaust of ecstasy to the delight of Cthulhu, Tsathoggua, Ghatanothoa, Dagon, and more."

Carter rises, tipping over his briefcase, scattering its contents. "You're a charlatan! No … worse! An imposter!"

Nyarlathotep, paying no heed, sneers into the balcony. With a click of his wrist the audience rises, marionettes, on the ictus around Carter.

The crowd troops towards the rear exit, the current carrying Carter along as he feigns defiance.

"I'm not frightened! I'll never be frightened! Not of you!"

But he sure as hell is frightened.

Very frightened.

More so than the dozens who parrot him for empty solace, none of who look back at the stage to see that Nyarlathotep has been supplanted by a taller, leaner man with brilliant black skin, Caucasoid features, no hair or beard, and dressed in a formless dank garment of shadows, clasping the apocrypha in one hand and pointing at the balcony with the other.

Outside a faraway bell tolls and smoky-smelling breezes blow and the Beaux-Arts buildings look genuinely ancient in the gloaming. Concrete discolored, splotched with lichen, inscriptions weathered away. Dull and grimy windows cracked or missing glass. Standing oblique amongst the Quadrangle's weed-choked grounds like forsaken Roman tombstones in some forbidden Welsh wood.

As the procession tramps into the October country, heading north up Garrison Street towards the Miskatonic, Arkham proper appears its usual self until the streetlamps and houselights sputter and a greenish perigee moon reveals a state of decay. Loose pavement displaced with grass. Dilapidated vehicles, some on sides. To the east, the top of the West Church steeple is ragged, and, to the west, Christ Church's spire is missing. In the distance he hears the lapping of water.

Hundreds more people funnel into the procession at Lich Street.

Thousands more at Church Street.

The moonlight dissects them into formations, each marcher somehow knowing their destination, and each one pretending to laugh like the second mate of the *Pequod* at everyone else's trepidation.

As the marchers approach Main Street a column splinters leftward through a chocked gate of graven dolomite into a tapered alleyway beneath a tenebrous overcast, leaving an echoing moan in their wake.

A second column howls with insane hilarity as it advances past River Street into a tunnel leading beneath the Miskatonic to some haven of eternal night, three crimson glimmers glaring as one out of the pitch.

One last column progresses into the country, bearing Carter past cleft ground and trackless evil snow swept asunder towards a mad aurora.

Frigid gales carry the high, thin whining from the balcony, and within the anarchic rolls of the aurora Carter sees the blasphemous city with its strange towers, labyrinths of wonder, low vaults of lights, and bough-crossed skies of glacial flame. Then, like no dream before, the column continues carrying him towards the aurora. Something in the whining beckons his primal deeps as he looks up to see limitless space whirling over the city, where a quivering, anamorphous blight of nethermost confusion looms, its laughter hollow and sepulcher as shapeless bat-things flop and flutter like idiot vortices around the glittering being.

Then a sensation outside Carter's nightmare disrupts. If translated into words, Carter hears: *"Collect your thoughts! Bridle the fluting! Or die lost in your sleep!"*

Carter stirs from the nightmare as well as his stupor when a commotion erupts in the corridor outside his room. Peering through the detention door's sliver window, he spies two interns strapping a new arrival to a gurney: a ruddy, wiry outdoorsy type, about seventy, with deep-set mahogany eyes, bushy slate-colored eyebrows, and a bristling beard reaching his breast. Clutched in his right hand is a thick, well worn paperback, the arrival's fingers digging into the cover and hiding its title. The thrashing newcomer growls, "Jump high! I'm gonna jump high!"

"Notify the on-call!" the senior orderly tells the other. "Tell him Slaader's having a paroxysmal event! I'll give him a bolus of sodium amytal, but should we take him to the crisis ward?"

Carter hears this while focusing on the ranting patient: "I've gotta find and kill the thing that shines and shakes and laughs! I'm gonna jump high in the air! Jump high and burn anything that stops me!"

4

"Dr. Halsey is on his way up."

Dr. Waldron thanks the orderly as he reviews test results on a tablet for the twentieth time. The more he looks, the queasier the medical director of the Miskatonic University Student Health Center feels, and Halsey, dean of the M.U. Medical School, is perplexed as he reviews them. "When did Elliott first notice symptoms?"

"Right after spring break. Thought it was a stomach flu he couldn't shake, and he certainly exhibits some gastroenteritis symptoms. The poor kid was so dehydrated when he came in this afternoon, I'd have admitted him anyway for nasogastric intubation and observation."

"Dehydration might explain the persistent gray skin. Tests results so far certainly haven't revealed any chronic or late-stage diseases. It might also explain his occasional states of bewilderment. Only his blood oxygenation looks good, and this collagen brittleness vexes me."

"Hear, hear. That worries me, too, Allan. Elliott's EHR document nothing even resembling osteogenesis imperfecta."

"It could always be a recent onset. His signs don't correlate with any foodborne diseases I know." Glances up. "No spike in comparable cases reported within the last month?"

"Not in the tri-state area, New York metropolitan area, or the Delaware Valley, but we'll be notified if there is. Meanwhile, Elliott's parents are driving in from Providence. Should be here soon. I'll give them a medical interview, see if there's anything like this in their family histories."

"And he only visited Providence over spring break?"

"That's what they're telling me. Otherwise, he's been in Arkham."

"All right. Since we can't dismiss that Elliott hasn't contracted a new strain of norovirus yet, I'll give the CDC a heads-up. If it is new, let's pray it's not virulent." Halsey scrolls through the test results again. "You've been practicing longer than anyone I know, Doc. You recall ever coming across any diagnosis with similar signs?"

Waldron is cautious not to reply too quickly. "I keep thinking about something I might have read in an old university bulletin. Something to do with one of the farms in the west valleys before the reservoir went in. I'll go through my files, see if I can find it."

"Why don't you check with Armitage, too? I think the library preserved a lot of bulletins on microfiche." Halsey returns Waldron's tablet. "Whatever Matthew Elliott has, hopefully it's an isolated case."

The following morning, however, a steadily increasing number of patients begin visiting Arkham's doctor offices, clinics, and emergency services, including Eddie Upton.

"Started feeling bad last night?" pediatrician James Reinertson asks as he slides a temporal thermometer across the boy's forehead.

"Yes." Eddie sits limp against his mother in her lap.

"Eaten anything since dinner?" The boy's temperature is 102^0.

"No."

"Stomach hurt?"

"Uh-huh."

"Dull ache or sharp pains?"

"Really sharp."

Dinah elucidates as she strokes the back of her son's head. "He had diarrhea and was vomiting all night long. He hardly had any energy to begin with, but now he's exhausted. When he could sleep, he kept mumbling, like he was having bad dreams. And he's so pale."

The boy's gray skin tone is Reinertson's prime concern. "Have you been giving him fluids? Water?"

"He won't drink anything."

"Well, all signs indicate a virus, so we don't want him getting further dehydrated. Why don't you take him to St. Mary's? I'll call and order a saline IV. I'd also like to order some tests to confirm this isn't bacterial. In either case, the IV should help with his coloring and ease those stomach ails."

"You're admitting him?"

"Let's cross that bridge after the tests have been run." Reinertson looks at the boy who favors his mother but acts so much like his father up and down one more time. "Right now the best thing we can do is get fluids into him. If it is a virus, all we can do is let him rest and make him comfortable until the bug runs its course."

5

Harold Barnard is encouraged.

"It's good to see you improving, Randolph."

Carter is more diffident. "Am I really? What about the swamp and Harley's office? What about my nightmares?"

Barnard is undeterred. "What say we parse those, starting with your night journey? You yourself claim to harboring doubts concerning what may have actually taken place between the moments you broke your ribs and giving your statement to the Miami police."

"I've begun to wonder if I even went anywhere with Warren. The police couldn't find the cemetery much less the road in Big Cypress Swamp."

"My experience with wetlands is limited to hiking the New England-Acadian forests as a student, but a swamp is a swamp. Considering how long this Big Cypress necropolis has remained secreted, I wonder if there are many people who'd be able to locate it without Dr. Warren's apocrypha. As for that road … well … his detective friends have a vested interested in shielding their profiler, don't they?"

"You think they're lying?"

"I think the popular acronym is CYA. Randolph, do you know where Dr. Warren is at this moment?"

Carter's head swiveled back and forth.

"Neither do I exactly, but according to Miskatonic's Psych Department he's somewhere on the Arabian Peninsula. They also informed me that he shall be incommunicado for the foreseeable future, after being granted an immediate sabbatical earlier in the afternoon you were found in his office."

"But I saw Harley! It was five o'clock! I heard the evening whistle! We talked!"

"And all this happened right before you saw that pharaoh?"

Without losing a beat: "Nyarlathotep only looks like a pharaoh."

Just as swift: "Aren't you splitting hairs?"

Carter realized he was and laughs for the first time in weeks.

"That's more like it! It's the well-adjusted man who can laugh at himself and recognize humor in unfortunate situations."

"Thank you … I think."

"You and I and many of Dr. Harley Warren's peers know that he is an ungovernable self-aggrandizer and inveterate exploiter. It's possible he stumbled across some significant discovery with your assistance and the aid of an apocrypha whose canon was written in Arabia. Now, lo and behold, Dr. Warren has taken off for Arabia after abandoning you here."

Carter wiggles in his chair, embarrassed. "I'm not saying he's incapable of what you're suggesting, but why leave the TTE in my hospital room?"

"You never had it."

"But -- "

"Hear me out. There is no record of Warren ever visiting NCH Baker. There were also no nurses on duty that night fitting your description. In fact, the hospital doesn't issue purple scrubs. I therefore suspect this dark woman and the TTE—like the pharaoh-looking fellow in Warren's office—were manifestations of your nightmare, except these were vivid enough to integrate themselves into your memories."

This hypothesis provides the patient little comfort. "That sounds like insanity, Dr. Barnard."

"Temporary insanity borne by stress, Mr. Carter. Stress from overwork, from your research, and from cognitive dissonance. You yourself have admitted to craving Harley Warren's attention, desiring his approval, all the while wishing to quit him and rid yourself of his manipulative influence."

Carter cannot deny this is true.

"Dr. Harley Warren is a meat grinder, Randolph. This will probably come as cold comfort, but you're not the first person whose life he's upended."

"Yes, but most other people realize that after one semester."

Barnard fails to comprehend.

"A bad joke. I'm sorry. Well, it sounds as if I'm better off and should be grateful." So why did he want to bawl?

"Give yourself some time. Rest and recognition can be excellent therapies, too."

"I see." It is a lot to absorb, but an orison enters Carter's mind. "'So ye shalt not nede to be afrayed for eny bugges by night, ner fer arowe that flyeth by daye.'"

"What is that? A proverb?"

"The Psalm of Protection. 91:5. It was one of my mantras as a child. It's still recited during some Jewish exorcism rituals."

"I see. Well, apotropaic magic can be balm for the soul."

"I suppose. Who is Slater?"

The midstream switch confuses Barnard. "Who is …'? Do you mean Slaader?"

"Is that the patient who was admitted last night?"

"The fellow who roused you, you mean? How did you learn his name?"

"One of the interns bringing him in mentioned it."

"Oh. Well, Joe Slaader was transferred from Machen County Psychiatric in New York."

"What's wrong with him? He was shouting how he was going to kill some 'thing.'"

"Yes. Slaader is a woodsman. Makes his living as a tracker in the Catskills. And he has a lifelong history of slipping into trances. They begin by him describing some sort of ethereal kingdom, then veer into tantrums over being somehow wronged and avenging himself."

"That sounds rather grandiose." Carter sounds harsher then he intends, startled that Slaader is likewise haunted by visions of an otherworldly realm and a persecutor.

"In any case, he hasn't long to live, I'm afraid."

"He's ill?"

"Not really. He has a strong heart, but his pulse is weak, his breathing is shallow, and he's lost fifty pounds in as many days. Slaader's just lost the will to live."

Frightened for himself, Carter asks, "Why? Have his spells grown so horrible?"

"No. More than likely it stems from his having beaten a man to death during a recent seizure. One of his relations and a childhood friend."

6

"Everybody in Arkham is worried about the flu."

It is twelve-thirty in the afternoon and for the third day in a row The White Ship has failed to draw a respectable lunch crowd. As Elton mostly keeps busy cycle counting behind the bar, a scattering of students imbibe in the free Wi-Fi, lattes, and ready to eat pastries like caramel shortbread and lamington, while Gilman and Derby split Cheese Frenchees and wets at The Shipwright Circle's favorite table, near the front door by the arched warehouse picture window watched over by a portrait of William Clark Russell.

"I hear you," Gilman tells Derby. "I've washed my hands so much they're raw."

"Same here. It's bad enough that more people are falling ill every day, but, if you contract it, it doesn't seem to want to let you go. At least that's the way it seems with Eddie."

"Poor Dinah and Daniel. They must be going through hell."

"I think Hell would be kinder. Dinah lives at St. Mary's for all intents and purposes, and Daniel is getting that way. He's always been able to alleviate problems by working, but not this time. I wish there was something I could do."

A new voice: "You can come with me."

Derby looks beside the table. "Asenath? I didn't see you come in."

"Me, neither," Gilman seconds, in spite of having an excellent view of the entrance and sidewalk outside the window.

Waite notifies Derby: "I am going to Innsmouth for a few days."

"Why? What's wrong?"

"Nothing. I'm taking advantage of the opportunity to visit."

"What about your classes?"

"I'm in good standing with all my professors, all of whom have voluntary attendance requirements. Not that it matters. The university will certainly be suspending classes soon."

One of the other students: "They ought to. My classes are all emptier than this place."

Elton comments from the bar: "You know, new flu strains seem to crop up every other year in Southern Australia. The bloody place is like an incubator. I can't recall a bug like this, though."

"Well, it's obviously an influenza epidemic. If the University suspends classes or not, I bet it won't be long before local or state authorities quarantine Arkham. Splitting while the splitting's good sounds prudent."

"Quarantines never averted infections in SA, but, if things keep going the way they are, some surrounding towns could quarantine themselves, the way they did in Mississippi, Alabama, and Florida during the 1878 Yellow fever epidemic. That might help."

Waite: "I doubt Innsmouth will initiate such a shotgun quarantine. People there don't get ill." Simpers at Derby. "Many of us have even gotten out of the idea of dying." Sterner. "You can't say the same, Edward, so I want you to join me."

Gilman stage-whispers, "I do think she's worried about you, bub."

Waite: "Haven't I made that clear?"

"Ignore Walter, Asenath."

"Are you coming?"

"You go. I'll have one less thing to worry about if you do."

"But -- "

"I'd never forgive myself if anything happened to Eddie and I was away."

"And you don't know how upset I'll be if anything happens to you."

Gilman injects: "Never fear. We've had our flu shots."

"Walter." Derby utters the name low and slow. To Waite: "You understand, don't you?"

Proceeding some stern stillness: "Let's say I comprehend and leave it at that." Pulling a folded slip of stationery from her clutch, she holds it out for Gilman. "I've been meaning to give you this."

He tentatively accepts. "You're not casting runes, are you?"

"I copied that from a transcript in my father's collection. He's never been able to completely translate it, but I thought it might help you with your research."

"Thanks. What is it?"

"Judge Hathorne ordered it transcribed from the walls of Keziah Mason's cell the morning she vanished."

"Are you … are you kidding me?" Unfolding the stationery, Gilman is confronted by a conundrum of algorithms mixed with curvilinear mathematic ideograms and abstract and figurative pictograms, many aquatic in design. "I've read something like this existed, but I thought it was just a legend."

Derby asks, "Do you understand any of it?"

"Some of the math. Maybe. It's heady stuff. Way beyond classical mechanics or anything Newton or even Liebniz were working on, which would fit with what Mason knew. It even looks weirder than the theorems MIT is designing to breed superior theorems."

"What about the writing?"

"All gobbledygook to me. I don't think I've ever seen cuneiforms like these. This is more in Carter's line."

"Agreed. For whatever it's worth, though, I've seen them before."

"Seriously? Where?"

"On some Innsmouth jewelry, for one place."

"And that is … ?"

"Jewelry its sailors received in trade from some South Sea islanders. Nobody knows which island exactly. Most Innsmouth jewelry was melted down for its gold-iridium alloy, but a few sailors sold a piece or two every now and again on the sly."

"Why doesn't anybody know which island it comes from?"

"It behooved the sailors to keep their honey hole a secret. Best estimate puts it somewhere east of Tahiti."

"Where did you see them?"

"The University Museum has a few pieces. They're utterly unique, and not just in composition. I've never seen their like in style or craftsmanship. Truly beautiful and truly weird."

"I've never heard about them."

"Well, the Museum doesn't exactly advertise they have any. Something to do with how the pieces were acquired, I think." Derby puts an index finger over his lips and shushes through his teeth. "I've got an in with a docent, though, if seeing them could help your research. The Historical Society of Old Newbury is also rumored to have a tiara boxed up somewhere that they used to have on display, and I'd be amazed if a few pieces haven't wound up in some private collections. Good luck finding those."

"Maybe Pickman could help there," Gilman chuckles. "He claims to know a thing or two about black market ghouls."

"Maybe he can help with the writing, too. Carter lost a bet when Pickman aced an undergrad paleographic class his sophomore year."

Gilman rubs the sides of his forehead. "Hasn't there been any academic research into this jewelry?"

"A few etymologists, archaeologists, and pseudoscientists have taken a stab at it, but what scholarly papers exist don't amount to much. You're welcome to anything I've collected on the subject, though."

"I'll take it. So where else did you see this writing?"

"On the island."

"I thought you said nobody knows what -- "

"Not that island! Cold Island." Arkham's own island between the bridges on West and Garrison Streets. "I've seen some of these pictographs and designs carved on a couple of large rocks near the stone chamber." A megalithic structure near the island's center. "They've been as much a mystery as the petroglyphs on the Judaculla Rock in North Carolina, but perhaps what Mason wrote can help crack the code." Derby starts to ask Waite more about the transcript, but: "She's gone."

Gilman looks where Waite stood. "I didn't see her leave."

"Without telling me good-bye?"

"Well, she's mad at you."

"No, she's not." Derby's lips pucker then sink to one corner of his chin. "I mean, she said she understood."

"That's not what she said. Tell me, does she lose many disagreements?"

"No. Not with me or anybody."

"Then maybe it's time she did. It'll put some hair on her chest. Yours, too. Still," Gilman holds up the stationery, "I owe her big time."

Outside The White Ship, Waite stands conflicted on the reconditioned boat slip as she watches the Miskatonic roll past on its way to Massachusetts Bay and the Atlantic. Asenath's substance—her very DNA—aches to be with Derby nearly as much as it yearns to wade into the river and swim far below. At the same time that Waite's mind—the body's cognitive faculties—merely respects Derby and possesses no craving for Adam's ale.

"Mind over matter," Waite whispers.

"Can be a tricky proposition," adds someone.

Waite turns to find a gentleman of indeterminable middle years smiling next to her. "I didn't hear you."

"I said -- "

"I mean I didn't hear you walk up."

The gentleman is wearing a tailored charcoal three-piece suit with matching shirt and black tie that would have been too youthful if his sharp figure did not cut the lay of his clothes with astonishing vitality. His dark eyes, thickish brows, hookish nose with nostrils that curve back to form a *v*, and meticulous salt-and-pepper mustache and beard evidence culture and intelligence, while the stranger's high flat temples, fixed mouth, and long and bony jaw resemble a wolf, intimating something feral lurking within the highbrow. Waite fully expects the silver top hat walking stick with black shaft the gentleman carries to conceal a rapier. The stranger frightens Waite even as the musk of danger resonates with the woman's essence.

"My apologies, but I've admired your father's work for quite some time. My name is Robert Sudyam."

"Of Red Hook?"

"Why, yes." Suydam, pleased, flashes his canines. "You know me?"

"I can't avoid you! My professors in medieval metaphysics invariably assign at least three of your articles on medieval superstition to their reading list."

"That's flattering! Who would have thought Miskatonic University would consider an old man from Flatbush to be such a profound authority?"

"Ephraim Waite does, too, although, I must confess, you don't look anything like your reputation." The woman takes the opportunity to appraise Suydam again.

"Yes, well, blame it on a change in lifestyle. I am not quite the recluse I once was, although I can't say I've completely forsaken solitude. Many a person's ills can be solved if he learns how to sit alone in a room." Another smile. "I only wish I could thank your father for his kind opinion, which, I assure you, pales in my admiration for him. I was terribly saddened to hear he passed away, and with so little warning. It must have been a shock." Suydam appraises Waite. "You know, I've only seen your father in photographs, and if they did him any justice then I see a lot of him in you."

"I'll take that as a compliment."

"Please do."

The woman blushes. "Are you here visiting family?"

"Oh, no, my relatives have far too little patience to abide with me. I came to Arkham for research. The university library really is unparalleled when it comes to some of its collections. I was also hoping to visit a couple of residents to extend an invitation to a join a cosmopolitan group of likeminded scholars to which I belong. Unfortunately circumstances and this outbreak are forcing me to cut short my visit."

"Hopefully you'll be able to return soon."

"That's my hope, too."

"Do I know any of these residents?"

"I think so. One in particular: Edward Derby."

Waite straightens and cocks her head. "My Edward?"

"From what several of the library's staff tell me, yes, your Edward. Edward Derby is a laureate in waiting, and we can provide the encouragement he requires to meet his creative and intellectual potential, in exchange for which our circle would be enriched by his membership."

"'Circle'? Does your group have name?"

Suydam appears bemused by the concept. "We're not really the types for frivolity, but, if our company had a name, it might be The Curwen Circle."

* * *

7

Herbert West draws solution from a vial into a syringe.

"Subject's TOD was approximately one hour ago, so at least a minimal of ischemic brain injury is to be expected. Therefore administering thirty mils of reagent via intraocular injection. Based on previous trial, expectation is any resulting reanimation will likely be primarily limited to gross motor skills."

The suspect, a seventy-four year old Caucasian male, lies on a dissecting table in the university's anatomy laboratory. As West spreads its eyelids to expose its left eye, another medical student splits his time watching the injection and watching out for Campus Security.

"Injection at 01:58." West pauses his digital dictation portable recorder as his accomplice inquires, "What if Security returns?"

"Security assisted us with transporting the subject down here. Remember?"

"But what if they got suspicious and are checking up on us?"

"Check with whom? The entire staff at St. Mary's is overtasked tending to living patients; otherwise we never could have relieved the hospital of this dead one. And why should Security be suspicious? What could be more natural than two medical fifth years examining a corpse in a dissecting room?"

"They won't think it's so natural if they come back and see your reagent kick in."

"What they'll think is the subject was misdiagnosed as deceased; a natural mistake considering the current hurly-burly."

"Only there's nothing natural about this particular to-do."

"You don't believe that." West feels the cadaver's wrist for a pulse then listens to its chest with a stethoscope. "From theory to trial, everything about this is natural. Better yet, it's empirical. We will succeed because reanimation is achievable."

"And never mind the ethics."

"Ethics is about truth and following that truth regardless where it takes you."

"Ethics is more than truth values. It's about how you get to the truth."

No reply.

"Herbert? This is where you tell me relevance … "

West activates his recorder. "At 02:10 the body became alive."

"Huh?"

The cadaver's eyes are open.

"Holy frijoles, it worked! I mean, the reagent worked the first time … maybe … but this time we can see it!"

West motions for silence as he dictates life signs, which are weak, and notes the subject's reinvigorated pallor remains as gray as it had been prior to death. Pausing the recorder, "Halsey's norovirus appears to be more persistent than the Dean."

"I'd call it pernicious. Look at his face."

The subject's countenance is contorted in terror with eyes fixated on the ceiling.

"Interesting. I expected some brain damage, but this seems more like neurogenic shock. That could explain the shallow breathing and hoary complexion; however … " West reexamines the subject. "I can't say why exactly, but I suspect the norovirus is affecting his mind more than any lack of oxygen." West waves his hands in front of the subject's eyes. "See? No recognition of motion whatsoever."

"His pupils react to light. He's obviously seeing something, even if we can't." Pause. "Perhaps he wasn't fresh enough?"

West taps a foot. "There is that." Pause. "Yes, we wasted precious seconds bringing the subject here. Nest time we will administer the solution as quickly as possible after somatic death." Slowly, a smile etches his lips. "This catatonia does not negate the fact that my reagent worked! It returned what's dead to life!"

8

"Eddie Upton died."

Carter clearly hears Pickman over the telephone, but it takes several seconds before his friend's words register. "Oh. I see."

During the week Eddie lay ill, nearly a dozen patients with the same signs passed away, beginning with the index case. As yet no cases have been reported beyond Arkham, which the governor had quarantined the day before through the Massachusetts Emergency Management Agency in hopes of preventing the spread of the unidentified contagion.

Pickman informs Carter that Eddie's funeral will not occur for a little while. "They've decided not to bury or cremate anyone who died from this flu until they verify the strain, so maybe you'll be out in time to attend. Of course, you can't return to Arkham until this quarantine is lifted, and it's a criminal misdemeanor if we're caught trying to visit you, otherwise I would have come told you in person."

"I know, and I appreciate that."

When the conversation ends, Carter returns to the common room to try to lose himself in mind-rotting television, but his thoughts whirl like a dog chasing its tail.

What could have happened?

Why did it happen?

Carter had been worried about Eddie, but, since the last he heard there were no complications such as pneumonia or myocarditis, he presumed Eddie's eventual recovery was a foregone conclusion.

As his thoughts reel Carter finds himself glancing around the room and occasionally trading ambivalent glances with Olmstead.

The news is tragic, but why does it bother him so? Tragedy is no stranger to Carter, who agreed with Bertrand Russell that Man's origins and growth, hopes, fears, loves, and beliefs are outcomes of an accidental collocation of atoms. As a boy, Carter would find solace in fantasies of nightly excursions to strange and ancient cities beyond space, but, with the onslaught of age and education, logic and analysis supplanted his childish dreams. Carter long ago accepted that the only beauty is in harmony and that everything—including himself—is a product of causes with no prevision of the end they are achieving. The earth, much less the universe, does not revolve around the needs and wishes of Man. In the end the temple of all Man's achievements will inevitably be buried beneath the debris of a blindly impersonal cosmos in ruins. "Gifts of God" or "God's doing" is just chance or fate, and when it comes to things like moral causality the Mesopotamians were closer to the truth than the ancient Hebrews, with the exception of King Solomon in Ecclesiastes. All is vanity with no more substance than a puff of wind.

So why did Eddie dying bother him?

Why can't he stop imagining Dinah and Daniel beside Eddie's deathbed as they try to comprehend life without their child?

Why should it matter so much to him?

As the impact of Eddie's loss intensifies, Carter retreats to his room to try to sleep. Failing that, he thinks about his mother, who, like his father, died at the Massachusetts Hospital School. For the first time since her passing five years ago, Randolph Carter cries, eventually drifting off sometime after midnight.

Sometime after that he hears the once-familiar beckoning cry of the willows and the whisper of night winds.

Carter knows he is sleeping, but is unsure he is dreaming.

All that happens feels real. Positive. True.

He is floating in an empty abyss. No water. No air. Pure space, devoid of light, and, for the first time in years, there is no ringing in his ears.

Then a translucent glimmer, faint and flickering as a firefly, turns steadier, draws nearer.

He is unalone.

The luminance, devoid of formal shape, is undoubtedly an entity and without doubt Eddie Upton. He and the luminous thing travel in tandem from the place of darkness past the hither stars as the firmament returns.

The sky fills with stars swelling to dawns bursting into a seething chaos of roseate and cerulean splendor.

He and the luminous thing pass glittering nebulae and silvery coruscations unknown and unbound by man, until, from out of a vortex, a way is revealed.

Resplendent valleys and prodigious meadows leading towards a marvelous city spread out before them, with mystery hanging over the city as clouds about a fabulous unvisited mountain. Even from this distance Carter discerns temples, colonnades, and arched aqueducts of veined marble interspersed among expansive squares with silver-basined fountains of prismatic spray, aromatic gardens, and broad thoroughfares marching between exquisite trees, blossom-laden urns, and ivory statues in gleaming rows, while red roofs and aged perched gables harboring grassy cobbled lanes ascend steep bluffs towards the north.

He had been this way before. In what cycle or incarnation, whether in dream or in waking, he had known this awesome and momentous place he could not recall; but the poignancy and suspense of almost-vanished memory, like that of a far, lost home, calls up a far-forgotten first youth when wonder and pleasure lay in all the mystery of days, unclosing fiery gates towards further and surprising marvels.

Eddie continues to the city, but the bondage of dream's tyrannous gods restrains him as Slaader's voice speaks: *"Gird your loins, boy."*

Carter sits up.

Tears sop his face.

Looks every which way, but he is alone.

Abandoning his room, Carter makes his way unnoticed to Slaader's room, where the macerated tracker is restrained to the bed. Carter notices the thick paperback on the nightstand and sees it is *The Count of Monte Cristo* as Slaader stares at him with intelligent determination.

Carter asks: "Did you call me?"

No answer, but Carter feels a tickle inside his ears.

Again: "Did you call me?"

Slaader still doesn't speak, but nonetheless answers: *"Misfortune is needed to bring to light the treasure of the human intellect."*

Carter slaps palms over his mouth to muzzle a scream, then, "How … ? How did … ? Who … ?"

"How I speak or who I am changes nothing, so why be afraid?"

Carter has no response for that.

"I am an entity like you become during dreamless sleep."

Carter remains quiet.

"How little the earth self knows life and its extent. How little, indeed, ought it know for its tranquility."

Not understanding what is happening, or unsure he wants to understand, Carter insists, "Tell me who you are."

"'Shall a faultfinder contend with the Almighty?' As you wish. Soon enough there will be nothing left of me but a corpse, so I may as well declare to you, and you may as well question me."

A pandemonium of scenes connect with Carter's mind and bring him to the outlands of madness as a limitless confusion of beings parade past, infinite in their multiplicity, monstrous in their diversity, drifting from world to world, universe to universe, until Carter is unable to distinguish betwixt them and himself. And throughout all this agony and all this dread he hears: *"There is much beyond the wall of sleep, Randolph Carter, for those who care or dare to look."*

9

Allan Halsey is in a bitter mood.

For the first time in forty years the dean is working resident hours, and has been since it became apparent that the virus, or whatever they were battling, is growing increasingly virulent. To make matters worse, every immunologist and epidemiologist at St. Mary's and the M.U. Medical School are stymied by what they are calling Elliott's Bug. There had been a glimmer of hope of identifying EB when Waldron and Henry Armitage located the university bulletin along with a coroner's report regarding a wasting disease that struck the Nahum Gardner farm nearly a century earlier; however, in spite of sharing some similar symptoms, more numerous differences made it apparent to Halsey that whatever had afflicted the Gardners is unrelated to Arkham's current scourge.

For one thing, many of the Gardners's neighbors and nearly a dozen Miskatonic professors visited the farm at the time, but the Gardners were the only persons definitively afflicted. What's more, a good number of the Gardner livestock was infected, as was some of the local wildlife along with some nearby crops and vegetation, but to date EB had not infected any fauna or flora in Arkham. The Gardner Strain likewise progressed much slower than EB and produced more dramatic physical deterioration. Even if EB and the Gardner Strain had turned out to be more analogous, the source of the Gardner Strain had never been identified. The coroner's report hinted that "some kind of effluvium" several witnesses had seen issuing from a meteorite that impacted beside the farm's well the previous summer was the likeliest culprit, but proving the medical examiner's conjecture at this late date was impossible, since 1) every meteorite sample brought to the university for examination inexplicably disintegrated within a few days, 2) lightning strikes obliterated the meteorite soon after its arrival, and 3) the Gardner farm and several thousand surrounding acres had recently been submerged by the West Valley Reservoir.

As exhausted as Halsey is, he is more frustrated he also has to contend with an attitude metastasizing amongst his colleagues and students that they should only treat the symptoms of EB patients until the virus is identified or runs its course.

"It's a matter of provisions," is how one associate dean rationalized it. "Even before the quarantine we were being forced to alter preferred treatment procedures due to shortages in everything from generic drugs to saline thanks to the GPOs and PMAs. It's prudent that we conserve our remaining supplies until we are certain how best to employ them."

Such arguments sound more like John Hardwig and less like Hippocrates to Halsey. Not that it matters. So long as he is dean he controls the key to the medicine cabinet, and—relying on recent reports from the Korean Society for Infectious Diseases and the Korean Society of Chemotherapy—he plans to continue prescribing 150 mg of antiviral agents such as Oseltamivir twice daily to his EB patients. Halsey also is relying on reports by the World Health Organization and the Center for Disease Control citing the need to continue antiviral treatment in severe influenza cases until the patient shows signs of recovery, even if it means extending past the standard ten day limit if the virus remains severe or progressive.

"Are you sure this is our best course, given the uncertainty these patients are suffering from influenza?"one of Halsey's brightest students, Herbert West, had inquired that evening.

"Their signs are similar enough."

"That's debatable, Dean, but, setting that aside, aren't you concerned with potential damage? *Nil nocere.*"

"I am, but there's no view to injury or wrong-doing here."

"No, sir, I never meant to imply -- "

"That said, I think we can also agree that doing nothing will definitely cause the greatest of harm: death. That outweighs any concern for potential damage."

"Yet -- "

"I will use treatment to help the sick according to my ability and judgment. That is how I practice medicine. You're free to choose a different path, Mr. West, but please don't expect me to impart precept or any other instruction if you do."

Halsey should not have jumped on West like that. West is a notorious dialectic, always questioning, always wanting to know more, traits that Halsey admired. Granted, Halsey was near the end of his rope and hardly in a Socratic mood, but that was no excuse for failing a student who meant no harm.

Driving home later that morning around three to finally grab a bite and forty winks, Halsey finds himself fixating once again upon a märchen his young mother told him about an invisible giant. Blind, pitiless, yet without malice, the giant brings plague to a kingdom grown too worldly in every way. Only an innocent maiden sees the approaching giant—a vast shadowy form covered in a great misty shroud—and only the city's eldest denizen—a man old enough to recall more trusting times—believes her. The pair risk their lives helping their stricken and often ungrateful neighbors, and his mother's description of the plague disturbed Halsey enough that he still carries it in his memory: "So many people died that one began to wonder that so many were left." One day the old man falls ill and the maid implores the giant to take her instead, but the dying man, soothed by her entreaty, tells the maid that we must give that which is dearer to us than our lives for the good of others. As the maid mourns her friend the giant departs the city, leaving these words drifting upon the wind: *"Innocence and devotion save the land."*

"If only."

Continuing east on Pickman Street, Halsey spots West walking south on Garrison Street with another resident toting a medical backpack. Pulling over to the curb, he waits for the students, calls them over, and tells West, "I'm sorry about earlier tonight."

"Dean?"

"I shouldn't have barked at you. Worse, I questioned your motives. That was uncalled for and very unprofessional. You were right to question and I hope I've done nothing to discourage that in the future. Please accept my apology."

"That's ... well ... that's ... of course, sir, but it's not necessary. Everyone knows how hard you've been working. It's good to see you taking a break."

"That's kind of you to say. Are you two heading back to St. Mary's?"

"No, sir," West's companion chirps. "We're off duty but on-call through tomorrow."

"Well, be sure to rest up. Job stress can sneak up on you." Halsey waves good night and pulls away.

"What do you know about that?" the second student asks.

"I confess I wasn't ..." West points. "Something's wrong."

Halsey's Corolla Sedan is slowing down and swerving towards a STOP sign at the Parsonage Street intersection. Gradually rolling up the curb, the Corolla bumps into the U-channel signpost, bending it backwards but unable to progress any further.

"Brake lights never came on!"

West runs to the Corolla. His companion follows. They open the driver and passenger doors. Halsey is unconscious and slumped, his seatbelt's shoulder strap preventing his head from hitting the steering wheel. West feels for a pulse then listens to Halsey's chest. "His heart stopped."

"Sudden cardiac arrest."

"You think?" West is already unfastening the seat belt and the students transfer Halsey to the hellstrip. West begins CPR to try to keep blood moving to the heart and brain. "Is there an AED in his car?"

The companion is already checking, grabbing the keys to look in the trunk. "No." Pulls out smart phone. "I'll call the trauma center."

"No! Defibs are only fifty-fifty effective with SCAs. Come here." When his companion is in reach, West yanks him down to grab the backpack and unzip it. "Take over CPR."

"What -- ?"

"I'll be damned if I'm going to be remembered as the student who let Dean Allan Halsey die."

"He was dead when we got here! And if we don't ..."

West pulls out a syringe and the vial of reagent.

"Herbert! No!"

Jabs needle into vial. "A normal dose to begin with."

"That's not even a last resort!"

"Then do it Old School and call for a defib. We're wasting time." West spreads the lids to Halsey's left eye. The other student grabs his wrist, but West twists free and shoves. Before his companion can recover, West injects the reagent. Tossing the syringe and vial into the backpack, West takes out a digital stethoscope and commences CPR again. "Pull up the app and start recording."

The companion does as told, caught between horror and fascination.

After about a half minute West breaks off CPR to listen. Concentrates. Ignores perspiration rolling into his eyes from his forehead.

The other student gasps, transfixed by the app. "H-e-r-b-e-r-t."

For the second time that night, a smile etches West's lips.

Gerber recognizes the intruder but has never seen anything like this before.

CHAPTER THREE

THE SCOURGE, GRINNING AND LETHAL

1

Patrolman Davis eyes the two grad students.

Number One is the Alpha. Between five feet five and six. One thirty-five soaking wet. Tow-headed. Glasses. What he lacks in mass he makes up for in hubris.

The Beta is the paradigm of the classic witness description: mid-twenties, brown hair, brown eyes, average height, average weight, average looks.

If these two aren't more than friends then something is off-kilter with the universe. The pair certainly shares some secret, and, judging from the young men's bruises and the shamble that used to be the Alpha's apartment, Davis would wager it includes an unrequited pique for some rough stuff.

"So you and your friend have no idea who did this?"

"We told you, no. We never got the chance to ask the man's name."

"Your landlady says she saw you two outside around three-thirty, propping up what appeared to be a third man who seemed to be in his cups. Is that who moved your furniture?"

"Pardon?"

"Is that who did all this damage?"

"It was, and the time sounds correct."

"Your landlady also says things were quiet up here until around three forty-five. Does that sound correct?"

"I'd say three-fifty."

"So what were you doing that you never got the chance to ask this guy's his name?"

"We were just helping him. He was really drunk." This from the Beta, practically on cue.

"What made you want to help? You two with The Salvation Army?"

"He was in pretty rough shape when we found him." Beta appears to think this through some more. "Well, he looked like he was in rough shape." A little more thought. "We're medical students."

"So you said, right before you said you were walking home after pulling a three-day shift at St. Mary's."

"We were. Except I live on Washington."

"So what's your address?"

Beta recites his apartment and building numbers along with phone number, and then asks, "Are we in trouble?"

Alpha looks as if it is taking all his restraint not to groan or shake his head.

Davis: "I can think of three scenarios off the top of my head that make more sense than your story, two of which are frowned upon by the Massachusetts Criminal Code."

Alpha: "We did nothing immoral. We came to the aid of another human being. That is the truth."

"All right, but, next time, maybe take any strangers you want to aid to St. Mary's or call 9-1-1. Look at this place! Look at you! I'm thinking you got off lucky. The people who called this in thought you were reenacting the shower scene from *Scarface* in here."

Neither student gets this gist of Davis's analogy.

The patrolman's partner, Officer Wolverstone, returns to the living room after searching the other rooms. "Well, our unsub definitely jumped out the bathroom window. You can see where some bushes broke his fall."

"'Broke his fall'? We're on the third floor!"

"Facts is facts. Maybe this guy was doping instead of drinking. I mean, something's got his adrenaline going. He didn't just bust through the window, he halfway yanked the frame out of the wall."

"That won't please the landlady." Davis looks at the students. "Okay, I get you're hesitant to press charges, but can you think of anything to add to your description? Negro? Thirty or thirty-five? Six feet? One hundred ninety-five pounds? In good shape? White tee shirt with blue jeans and Reeboks?"

Alpha shakes his head. "If there was anything more, like a visible scar or tattoo, one of us would have noticed. We're trained to look for such things."

"Sure, but if you do happen to remember something else, call the station."

The patrolmen return to their squad car soon after. As Wolverstone buckles his seatbelt: "There's more going on here than meets the eye."

"Whatever happened didn't go down the way Heckle and Jeckle say it did." The sentence fades in volume with each word.

"Something wrong?"

The patrolman twitches. "How do you fall three stories without breaking your neck or at least your leg? And if this is just some three-way that got out of hand, why exit out a window?" Davis starts the car. "Maybe I've watched *The Night Stalker* too many times, but I'll feel better after we find this Six Million Dollar Man."

2

"I can't believe I let you talk me out here!"

Gilman is sitting in the stern of Elton's 1947 Grumman 15-foot aluminum canoe as he snarls back, "Nobody talks you into anything you don't want to do."

Pickman, in the bow, knows this is true, but opts to blame Gilman anyway as the Arkham Police Department patrol boat passes under the West Street Bridge after rounding the Miskatonic's knee.

"Keep in tandem or we'll just flounder." Unlike Pickman, whose nautical experience is limited to riding the Inner Harbor Ferry, Gilman grew up canoeing the Merrimack and other nearby rivers and lakes. Repeating "Paddle!" every few seconds to bring Pickman's forward stroke back in synch, Gilman goons to straighten the canoe and then Indian strokes until they run aground on Cold Island. "Grab the backpacks and paddles!" Gilman drags the emptied canoe fully out of the water before tilting it onto one side, deftly rolling it over his head, and leading the way into the woods.

The patrol boat passes the island. Pickman: "They're not stopping."

"Thank God."

"'Thank' …? I always took you for a Neo-Platonist, not a theosophist."

"Well, I always figured you for an Anabaptist, so back at ya'." Gilman conceals the canoe behind some forest shrubs and then removes his life vest to toss it in the boat. "Give me the backpack, Dirk Willems, and stow the paddles and your preserver."

"Aye aye, Plotinus." After this, "Seriously, I'd have sworn they saw us."

"Seriously, I did, too. I suppose the sunrise could have blocked us from their view, but you'd think they'd have radar. Maybe it's just easier to try to scoop us off the river later than put to shore and hunt for us now."

"Or maybe they aren't bothering boaters who aren't trying to leave town."

"What sort of optimism bias are you on? 'No unauthorized river traffic during the quarantine.' Them's the rules."

"If they were strictly enforcing that, I bet we'd be in a brig right now." Pickman leans against a tamarack to catch his wind. Peering across the river, "You know, that's not a bad view."

"It's the south side of Arkham. You see it every day."

"Never from this perspective. It's … more suggestive … from what I normally see at the MBTA station."

Gilman takes a gander. "The slope's more noticeable, I'll give you that. You can definitely see more businesses behind the River Street warehouses from here."

"You can also see The White Ship."

"You're right. I didn't notice that."

"That's why I'm here." Pickman sets his smart phone's camera to panoramic. "I'll take a snap to show Basil when we return his canoe." Reading off landmarks as he sweeps the phone: "The Crowninshield Place … Burying Ground … Witch House … campus … West Church and St. Mary's behind it … Daniel and Dinah's place." A stumbled silence; then, more softly, "Hangman's Brook … the old Carter place."

Just as softly: "Have you talked with them?"

Pickman lowers the camera. "Not since … I figured that they want to be left alone. For now."

"Yeah, me, too." Gilman thinks of something: "Carter knows, doesn't he?"

"I called him that night. I'd rather have told him in person; he's already dealing with enough. I'm not sure how he took it."

"You know Carter. Pretend like something doesn't matter even when it does."

"That is his modus operandi, but he sounded different. Almost vulnerable."

"Carter?" Gilman weighs this. "Well, the Uptons are the only people he's never minded showing that he likes, at least since I've met him." A little more thought. "You've known him a lot longer, though, right?

Switching topics: "So where are the stones?"

Gilman points northward. "This way, Tin Woodsman. We'll have to stray a little from the highlands to reach the heart of the island."

As they leave the river behind, Pickman notices, "It's gotten humid quick." This in spite of Arkham's mostly temperate spring and no rain since the night Carter was found in Professor Warren's office.

"From what Derby told me, this spot generally feels muggy."

Soggy detritus and O horizon clump to Pickman's hiking shoes. "'Moist' might be a better word." Runoff from inaccessible sloughs a few yards off rills over and runnels under the path in several places. "Did Derby mention anything about the Miskatonic flooding this place lately?"

"Cowboy up. When did a little sweat and condensation hurt anyone?"

"Just because I can't think of an example off the top of my head doesn't mean they haven't." The trees are also different than in Arkham. Larches dominate, more than a few of them coiled, grossly entwined, or lacerated by lianas and hairy vines. As the men draw deeper into the woods, persistent skitters in the needle canopy overhead and poppings like dropping chestnuts through the limbs and understory pester Pickman. He had not heard a bird or a bug since their arrival and the stillness of the heavy air, plus numerous fallen trees—snapped as if something gigantic often came this way—increases his unease. After what feels like several minutes of marching, Pickman asks, "This isn't the way to the Micmac burial ground, is it?"

Gilman sniggers. "Derby warned me it can feel creepy here at times. Kind of like you're out of sync with your surroundings or time. I bet that explains the lack of litter. A place like this should draw frisky, thirsty young 'uns like moths, but even campers and fishermen don't come here often. I kind of like it, though."

"Groovy. So are we almost there yet, Westley? This is a long walk for such a small island."

Gilman wags his head. "Really? No, shouldn't be much longer."

Pickman pulls out his smart phone to check the time and sees they have been walking less than four minutes.

To himself: "Really?"

Pulling up the south Arkham panorama to give his mind a locus, Pickman fixes on The White Ship, where he passed the previous night sipping Pamplemousse and contemplating the weird things happening in Arkham with Basil. Bad as the quarantine was, Dean Allan Halsey was missing, and, a few hours after Halsey's abandoned car was found on Parsonage Street that morning, the corpse of a mysophobic suicide was discovered having been partially eaten in the deceased's Crane Street home. Gilman arrived to borrow Elton's canoe, and, in the process, requested Pickman join him.

"Why should I risk padding my rap sheet just to traipse around that spit of land and get covered with cleavers? Take heed of what Eliot wrote about 'old stones that cannot be deciphered.'"

Gilman repeated what Derby told him.

"Edward's the gift that keeps on giving. Like a bad reputation. Listen, I'm no expert on petroglyphs or pictographs. I only took that class to satisfy an elective."

"But I need that knowledge base. Besides, what else is there to do with classes cancelled for the time being?"

"Several things I'd rather do leap like satyrs to my mind."

"*Rather* being the optimum word. If any of those Bacchanalia were options, you'd be doing them rather than sitting here."

"'A man can hope.' Besides, this falls into Carter's bailiwick, not mine."

"He's indisposed. Remember?"

"Then wait until he's disposed. Okay? Patience is a virtue, Prudentius."

"Not right now it isn't, Evy."

Elton interceded: "Walter needs your help because his mathematical muse is turning into a monkey on his back. Like when an artist's inspiration turns into an obsession."

"Oh? Now, see, there's something I can empathize with."

Gilman: "So you'll come along?"

"I didn't say that."

Elton: "Don't be a sook. I'd like to hear what you might find out. So what if I throw in brekkie along with my tinny? How does egg and spam sandwiches with a couple of cold ones sound?"

Gilman: "I'd prefer a vegemite sandwich."

"Don't be a turkey, Walter, and Mr. Buffett warned you about the dangers of warm beer and bread."

Pickman chuckles at the memory as Gilman leads them into a clearing, announces, "We're here," and points towards a sentinel—the largest and most contorted tamarack on the island—overlooking a stone chamber. Big bare roots sink like talons into the side of a ditch leading towards the chamber's entrance, a jarring gap reminiscent of the socket of a yanked tooth. Most of the chamber lies under earth and duff with only a portion of the slab roof and a bric-à-brac of fieldstones assembled chockablock around the entrance visible. Standing near the ditch's access is a circle of six small sandstone boulders of roughly the same size and abraded with petroglyphs. A distorted shadow from the tamarack drapes the scene, and the only thing Pickman can think to do is snap a picture before asking, "What's inside?"

Gilman appraises each boulder as he answers: "A fifteen-foot long tunnel leading to a beehive chamber. It's similar to ones built by Medieval Culdee Monks, but nothing unusual there. Most megalithic structures in this part of Massachusetts share the same floor plan. This chamber is the biggest, though. Eleven feet in diameter. Ten feet high."

"Somebody's done his homework. Any carvings?"

"No. Virtually no artifacts, either. Again, that's par for the course with stone chambers. Nobody can prove who built them, but most archao-astronomists figure this one was used to study the Pleiades and the summer solstice during the second half of Millennium One ACD." Looks up at the sentinel and then the sky. "Sure is a gloomy spot. I read that some folks say the sun doesn't seem to ever shine here."

"Well, my Naumkeag blood tells me there's something not right about this eyot. This spot especially. This looks like the kind of place that keeps its secrets."

"Listen to you! If you're spooked, you've got a better reason then ancestral intuition."

No reply.

"Go ahead. Take the Fifth. Scholars have been coming here for decades and not one has ever reported so much as feeling the creepy crawlies."

"Maybe none of them were looking for what you're searching for or brought along a potential Rosetta Stone."

"Which isn't doing anyone any good so long as you're over there and these stones are over here."

Pickman shakes his head. "And Carter says I'm mulish." Sighs. "Fine." Reluctantly joins Gilman. "But this is as far as I go. It's not like I'm going be able to decrypt anything."

"Let me worry about that."

"Fine." Looks at the stones. "So what do you see?"

"I'm seeing what you're seeing."

"Which is exactly the gutless empirical response I'd expect from an Einsteinian. We're not on *Wheel of Fortune*, Walter! Just describe what you see."

"Fine. I see pictographs interspersed with curved mathematical designs."

"Okay then."

"So what do you see?"

"I see picture painting."

"You mean this is just a bunch of art?"

Pickman shudders. "That is insulting on so many levels."

"Sorry." Gilman doesn't sound sincere.

"Look, writing is the most conventional form of picture painting. If you're going to comprehend the meaning of these markings, you need to appreciate them for what they are. *Appreciate* being the optimum word. Peel your eyes."

"Okay, sensei, I hear you. What is it that I'm not seeing?"

"First, very early writing, like petroglyphs, is semasiographic. Non-phonetic."

"Like mathematical and musical notations?"

"Also computer icons and emojis. Writing is a system of human intercommunication that uses conventional visible marks, but, in the very beginning, pictures served as a visual expression of ideas. Thoughts and feelings were communicated through visible signs before writing developed into a device for expressing linguistic elements. To quote Voltaire, *"L'écriture es la peinture de la voix."*

"Or, to quote Aristotle, 'Spoken words are the symbols of mental experience and written words are the symbols of spoken words.'"

"Carter would be so proud of you. Of course, he would have recited Aristotle in Latin." A wistful snort. "Anyway, this is my point. These carvings aren't attempting to talk. They're expressing ideas."

Gilman is sincerely confused. "Is that really an important difference?"

"I bet it was to Keziah Mason, if the stories about how she flew the coop are true." Silence, then, "I can go over technical stuff if you want, but I figure a physicist is already up to speed on things like the principle of positional value."

"Yeah, I am." Silence, then, "Do you think the stories about Mason are true?"

"Why not? She was never hanged."

"What about how she escaped? It's one thing to think she was some kind of late-blooming Ramanujan, but could she have really been a witch?"

Pickman's scowl is as hard as the sandstone, an expression Gilman remembers from The White Ship when Derby blurted about Pickman's ancestor.

"Oh, damn it, I'm sorry. I ... "

Pickman holds a hand up as his expression alters, becoming as undecipherable as the carvings as he stares at one petroglyph on the boulder nearest the chamber. Turning towards the entrance, he says something that sounds like *azimuth* to Gilman. Then: "If only civilization was safer than this place."

What do you mean?"

Points in the direction of the Miskatonic and Arkham. "'Yonder is the sea, great and wide, which teems with things innumerable ... and Leviathan which thou didst form to sport in it.'" Looks back at Gilman. "Maybe I am an Anabaptist. Just pray you never believe what I do when it comes to what's terrible and human ghosts." Then, walking towards the draw, "I'll wait over here until you're done, if you don't mind."

3

Randolph Carter is dreaming.

He floats once more down the abyss, and, like before, there is only silence as he descends like a winged being to the confines of infinity.

Once again, he is unalone. Slaader is waiting and tells Carter, *"Not many know what wonders are open to them in the stories and visions of their youth."*

Carter says nothing; waits to hear more.

"Children listen and dream but think in half-formed thoughts, so, later, when men try to remember, they are dulled and prosaic with the poison of life."

"Childish dreams become supplanted by logic and analysis."

"Not many that awake in the night know they have looked back through the gates of that world of wonders which was ours before we were wise and unhappy."

"Is that what waits beyond the wall of sleep?"

Slaader says nothing as the rift reappears, but this time Carter sees the familiar hills west of Arkham, including a high slope where a white gambrel-roofed farmhouse stands on a treeless knoll surrounded by a twisted-boughed apple orchard.

He recognizes the rise as Elm Mountain.

He recognizes the house as his people's rustic homestead.

And he recognizes himself, nine years old, as he runs from the farmhouse towards an upper timber lot. Recognizes and becomes that boy once more as he imagines the trees and hills forming a gate to an ageless realm of fauns and aegipans and dryads that is his true country. He runs higher—past hoary willows and lichen rocks—and higher—across a fast-running stream whose rumbling falls beckons unseen—and higher still—to a cave lurking amongst grotesque, glutted oaks.

He recognizes the cave as the Snake Den, and remembers being drawn to this shunned place that country folk associate with his forefather Edmund Carter, a wizard they believe fled here after escaping the shadow of Gallows Hill.

Panting as he catches his breath, young Carter pulls a flashlight and a huge tarnished silver key from his pants pockets. Trying to remember where he found the relic scrolled with cryptic arabesques as he passes through the black, forbidding orifice, something seems very confused. People say the Snake Den is deep, but Carter knows it goes far deeper than anyone suspects, having found a root-choked fissure in the furthermost corner. Wriggling through, he returns to a loftier sepulchral grotto whose ultimate wall hints of a monstrous pylon. Roaming his flashlight over the dank wall, Carter boggles at the suggestion of an arch and what could be a keystone and a stony bulge his fancy insists is a gigantic sculptured hand. Holding up the key, Carter senses an incalculable disturbance and confusion in Time and Space … and emerges from a stone chamber watched over by a tall, twisted larch. Instinctively dowsing with the key, he passes a stone circle, follows a re-entrant to a river, and recognizes he is looking across the Miskatonic at Arkham as it used to be. At River Street and its warehouses, including a vacant one belonging to Nicholas Brown and Company with a damaged boat slip. At the secondary businesses on Main and the main businesses on Church. At the Crowninshield House with homely lights aglow inside. At steeples and landmarks, including old St. Mary's, the white church yet to be torn down to give way to its namesake hospital. At the streets lined with willows, maples, poplars, ash, and tupelos, and then the hills with great elms, winding roads, gnarled orchards, and vine-grown stonewalls.

"There is much to learn for those who care or dare to look."

"I don't understand the difference."

"Principles and application. 'To learn is not to know; there are the learners and the learned. Memory makes the one, philosophy the other.' You possessed the key to the ivory gates, yet, over the years, the more certain you knew, the more you lost it. The Man of Truth, however, remembers all."

Carter, a young adult again, clutches empty hands as the rift shuts and he finds himself standing with Slaader on a windswept tableland on what could be the roof of a blasted, tenantless world.

"Here is where you start if you wish to reclaim it. Many journeys begin as well as end here."

In the furthermost distance is a rim of impassable peaks, the wind swarming over them hauntingly whining *tekeli-li* as Carter senses something awful behind the mountains watching them like eyes in darkness. "Where are we?"

"Asia. Antarctica. North of the dream realm. Or elsewhere. All that is certain about this place is that this is the cold waste of Leng."

Carter shivers. "*This* is Leng?" He recognizes the name from the *Necronomicon* as a place no healthy folk visit, just as he recognizes the squat windowless building of uncouth stones encompassed by crude monoliths of inhuman cut rising between them and the mountains. "And is *that* the monastery?"

"Wherein a way to the underworld is rumored to be found. So you know of the High-Priest Not To Be Described, who prays here to the Outer Gods and their Crawling Chaos Nyarlathotep? I once drew too close and barely escaped, so we shall keep this distance. From Leng, though, all journeys are possible, so let us begin ours now."

As Slaader speaks Carter notices something or someone in the monastery's entrance: an indescribably familiar watcher even though its lumpish figure is robed in yellow with red arabesques and its face is covered by a yellow silken mask. Then, in a whirlwind, a pilgrimage through incomprehensible Time and Space commences.

Randolph Carter miraculously leaps a gulf of years betwixt eons past and still to come as his spirit dwells with different branches of humanity, civilizations, and worlds: philosophers and generals, monks and kings, magicians and physicians, physicists and priests, commoner and chieftains, all with secrets and marvels to share. Carter even dwells in a place outside Space inhabited by glowing gases of unidentifiable color that study the secrets of existence and categorize him as coming from the infinity where form, matter, energy, and gravitation exist. Often throughout this odyssey Carter still senses he is being watched, and, on rare occasions, spots a shadow out of the corner of an eye of what appears to be a clawed, snouted being that seems somehow reminiscent.

Then he awakes—or thinks he has—as he calls for his mother. There is no answer and then he remembers that she has been in her grave for a quarter of a century, although her as well as his father's deaths ache as if fresh. Carter finds himself in his middle fifties and living alone in the home of his mother's family in Boston. Convinced of the hollowness and futility of reality, he has been musing more and more upon oblivion even as he spends his days refitting the home to the way it was during his boyhood and his nights in slumber that flicker with the vaguely awesome imminence of tensely clear pictures long forgotten from childhood. One night Carter remembers his father's father—dead almost fifty years—reciting their lineage to him, commencing with a Crusader who learned wild secrets from his Saracen captors, followed by the first Sir Randolph Carter, who studied magic when Elizabeth was queen, and Sir Randolph's heir Edmund, who sequestered a great silver key handed down by his ancestors inside an antique box prior to fleeing Arkham in 1692.

Then Carter's dream journey ends.

He awakes, returning from beyond the constellations, beyond light and darkness, and beyond Time. He stares at the ceiling, lying in his bed in the Hospital School, alone again yet overcome by the places he had been and the things he had seen. Giddy, he wants to shriek and leap up, but feels as unsteady and ignorant as a baby after the expanses and recesses and behemoths and leviathans from his vision of the night. Carter can tell by the electric illumination shining from the corridor through the detention door's window that it is night, but he is uncertain how long he has been away, his odyssey having stripped him of any distinctions between the Carter he was, the Carter he is, and the Carter he may become as Slaader's parting words ring in his mind: *"Having taught you a small part of what I know, a new passion may instill itself in your heart. Time will tell. Philosophy cannot be taught, and man is but man after all."*

4

Edward Derby is on the hunt.

Thanks to Drs. Armitage and Waldron the game is afoot, starting with the librarian asking Derby: "Do you know anything about a west valley farm owned by a Nahum Gardner?"

Something about the name did ring a bell, but Derby could not say why.

"The farm was situated in an area known as the blasted heath. The attenuated area's zero point, as it were."

Derby snaps his fingers. "A meteorite landed there? In the 1880s?"

"June of eighty-two." Armitage explains that a team of professors had studied the meteorite as he presents Derby with a thick expanding wallet. "Herein is a copy of the bulletin which presented their findings along with Xeroxes of anything else I could scrounge from our collections about the incident, including a coroner's report, eyewitness testimonies, and several newspaper articles."

"There's more in here then … did you say 'coroner's report'?"

"Yes. By November of eighty-four, Mr. and Mrs. Gardner and all three of their children had succumbed to some withering affliction that may have also infected the plant and animal life surrounding their property. The coroner, Dr. Thomas Aylesworth, suspected the meteorite was somehow responsible, at least for what happened to the family, but his evidence was more circumstantial than direct. Judging by his reputation, Aylesworth wasn't a doctor known for making unwarranted speculations. Quite the opposite."

As Derby riffles the wallet's contents, "Do you wish me to review this, sir?"

"Not just that. I agreed to help Waldron because we hoped what I found would assist local and state health authorities identify the illness plaguing Arkham."

Derby stops.

"I know your best friends lost their son ... your namesake ... to this scourge. Therefore I should say that I wouldn't ask this if there was anyone else we could entrust with this task. We've always been truthful with each other, Edward, and the fact you've been scarred by this tragedy makes you uniquely qualified to help us."

Derby clears his throat. "How?"

Armitage recounts how Halsey reacted to the information in the bulletin and coroner's report, "However Waldron is not ready to dismiss the Gardners as dead ends. Since there are no living eyewitnesses or extant meteorite samples ...and since the farm and blasted heath are cold underwater ... our only recourse is to find out how Patient Zero, Matthew Elliott, contracted his fatal illness to verify if a connection exists between the events. Poor Allan's opinion understandably carries a great deal of weight, so the health authorities are refusing to pursue this information I'm giving you any further. That said, Waldron is too busy and I'm too out of shape for such detective work, which is why I am asking you to be our Archie Goodwin."

Derby would have said no to anyone else. Eddie's death is still so painful. Even so, Derby is grateful to have something to occupy his thoughts, especially if it has even the remotest chance of ending the epidemic.

After spending the morning reviewing the contemporaneous material concerning the Gardner farm in the wallet, Derby proceeds to more recent content (surreptitiously provided by Waldron) starting with copies of Elliott's medical reports and case studies of subsequent EB patients including Eddie. Doing his best to ignore flashbacks of Dinah and Daniel's distress as local health officials searched their home and collected some of their dead child's belongings after the quarantine was implemented, Derby scrutinizes forensic photographs of Elliott's Boundary Street studio apartment and reads the lab reports conducted on clothing and bedding collected there. Deciphering enough of the reports to comprehend that the findings were inconclusive at best, Derby scrutinizes the photographs again and then asks Armitage to request a favor of Waldron.

Early that evening, Derby enters Elliott's apartment building carrying a goody bag of hospital supplies and a sterilized key Waldron borrows from Elliott's personal effects. Checking that no one is watching, Derby slips on a procedure mask and black nitrile gloves before unlocking Elliott's door, ducking under yellow tape put up by the Arkham Health Board, and closing the door behind him.

The apartment looks different from the photographs. Gone are the over-the-counter flu relievers, ear thermometer, nearly empty tumbler of water, and three remote controls that littered a Sauder end table beside the stripped pull out sofa. Also missing are MU Shipwrights sweat pants and a New England Patriots hoodie that had been wadded on the mattress along with a fleece pullover sweater and pleated corduroy pants that had been wadded nearby on the floor. The absent pants reminds Derby of the summary in one lab report that cited an analysis which had been unable to identify all the elements in some sort of oily green matter splattered on the cuffs, only water, carbon, calcium, nitrogen, and iron. To Derby's relief he finds books, magazines, assessor records, photocopies of historical newspaper articles, and notepads filled with Elliott's chicken scratchings that had been scattered around the bed now stacked on the dinette table. Sifting through the literature, Derby realizes that Elliott—an architectural major—had been conducting a historical survey on the Harris House on Benefit Street in Providence. Familiar with the old farm building's unlucky reputation, Derby is intrigued to discover that the original owner of the small tract the home stands on was a descendant of Jacques Roulet, the notorious vagabond from Caude, who, in 1598, was convicted of murder, cannibalism, and lycanthropy. Derby is even more intrigued to read how Elliott's great-uncle was helping with his survey. Pulling out his smart phone, Derby speed dials and waits to hear: "*Providence Journal.* Aldin Norton."

"Hi. It's Derby."

"Hey! You in Arkham?"

"Yes."

"Feeling okay? That quarantine still on?"

"I am, thank you, and it is."

"Man, that's nuts."

"Listen, since I'm stuck here, I need your help."

"Let me guess. Want me to air drop you some Pop-Tarts?"

"This is serious." Although grape Pop-Tarts did sound good. "Are you familiar with Dr. Elihu Whipple?"

"You kidding? Got a lead on him?"

"Not exactly. Were you aware that he's Matthew Elliott's great-uncle?"

"Really? Are the old guy disappearing and the kid getting sick connected?"

"That's something I'm trying to find out. Elliott was in Providence over spring break, and I have it on good authority he planned to explore the Harris House with Whipple during his stay."

"Harris House, huh? Who's the authority?"

"I'm not at liberty to disclose that yet. It could get me and some other people in hot water."

"Say no more. But you're sure? You have proof?"

"I have it in Elliott's own handwriting."

"Nice. But you don't know if they went through with it, right?"

"That's why I'm calling. Someone needs to check if they did."

"'Someone'?" A loud gulp. "You know, the word is a lot of people who lived in that spooky old place -- "

"'Spooky'?"

"It has a rep."

"I've never read where anybody's claimed it's haunted."

"It's shunned. Like I was saying, enough people living there since it was built have got sick and died that the owner can't even rent it out anymore."

"I know, but a lot more people could end up losing their lives here."

"Okay, I hear you, but if Elliott died because he went rummaging in there -- "

"We don't know if there's a connection. If there is, though, think of the clicks that story would get."

Slowly, enticed: "Yeah. Still -- "

"Look, stop at a drug store on the way and buy a surgical mask and gloves. I'll pay you back. Aldin, my best friends's son died from this. Help me, please?"

A long exhale, followed by longer silence, and then, "I so should have let you go to voice mail."

* * *

5

"How did I get here?"

As Chris Gerber makes his rounds of the Burying Grounds he aims his flashlight at the brick walkway more from habit than necessity. It is pitch-black out, but Gerber, a life-long Arkhamite, can walk the path with his eyes closed.

"How?"

Gerber is bone-weary and not because of the hour. He requested midnight-to-eight when Hadenfeldt Security hired him a decade earlier because he had worked the graveyard shift for most of his thirty years on the police department. What has him mumbling tonight and most nights lately is his situation: a lifelong bachelor with no children, few friends, and an inadequate pension for someone recently diagnosed with type-1 diabetes and a ninety-three-year-old mother he visits every week at the senior memory care center in Bolton.

"How in God's name did I get here?"

Fixating on that thought—his only his company most of the time—Gerber pays scant attention to a sliver of pale moonlight sneaking through the lush cloudage and almost misses the outline of a trespasser it casts on the hilltop on the north end of the Burying Ground.

Almost.

"What are you doing up there?" he calls.

The trespasser continues walking as Gerber trains his flashlight at the figure, but it remains obscured by distance. Judging by the stoop and shamble, the intruder is inebriated or elderly. Either way, this is probably not a vandal, but Gerber hollers louder and draws light trails with his flashlight until he catches the trespasser's attention.

"Hold up! Wait right there!"

Gerber steps carefully as he forsakes the walkway. New England legends claim that an intricate tunnel system—most probably built for smuggling prior to the American Revolution—exists beneath the Burying Ground, extending west to Hill Street and Hangman's Brook and north to River Street and the Miskatonic. Gerber has no idea if this is true, but he knows that an ever-expanding network of tunnels is being burrowed beneath the jumble of gravestones and tombs by an infestation of woodchucks. These excavations have exposed human bones in a few of the crumbling graves and made it increasingly risky to tread anywhere except on the brick paths. The last thing Gerber needs to do two hours before the end of his shift is snap a foot off at the ankle because some chucklehead wandered in from Church Street without noticing where he was headed. Gerber might not even be bothering with this chump if the trespasser was not so near the jagged pyramidal façade of the Pierce Tomb, a favorite bolthole for thirsty teenagers.

Set into the side of the north hill, the vault holds seven bodies, including a Civil War veteran and three tuberculosis victims. Its roof is level with the hilltop, making it inviting for anyone determined enough to burrow from the rear to break in and descend into the crypt using ropes. Most kids are satisfied with swilling some beer or other alcohol, but there have been a few exceptions, one of the most notable being the initial transgression in 1925. On that night something inspired the inebriated interlopers to don some of the decedents's togs and frolic about the cemetery's frog pond until they were arrested. This idiocy was outdone one summer sixty years later when six scallywags made several visits to the tomb, each time sharing adult beverages with their hosts by pouring alcohol down the cadavers's throats. Even more bizarre rituals were also rumored to have taken place, but no one, including the police, ever revealed what those might have been. Eventually the caretaker stumbled across evidence of these violations, and soon after the perpetrators began turning themselves in after the *Arkham Advertiser* reported above the fold on its front page how three of the tomb's occupants had "expired from a dangerous contagious disease."

"Imbeciles," Gerber grumbles as he reaches the hilltop. Before aiming his flashlight at the trespasser, the figure's cockeyed posture and the silhouetted suggestion of an unbuttoned suit coat remind Gerber of a movie he saw as a teenager at the 1-A Drive-In. As a nerd and his plain Jane sister visit their father's grave they spot some weird guy in a black suit shuffling towards them, at which point the nerd trills in a Boris Karloff voice, "They're coming to get you." Recalling the line sends a shudder up Gerber's spine as he lights up the trespasser.

"What the hell?"

Gerber recognizes the intruder but has never seen anything like this before.

The nauseous eyes.

Demonic savagery.

Face and teeth smeared with tarry crud and blood.

How the intruder sways like an ape but moves twice as quick.

Gerber unholsters his Glock 22 and shouts "Dean -- !" as the trespasser snares him.

Somersaults in the air with Gerber and lands on the guard.

Drives knees into ribs, splintering them.

Rips out Gerber's throat.

Then digs.

Some of what the trespasser scoops out will be carried away for later.

6

Arkham is in a panic.

Someone making a meal of a slightly stale corpse is troublesome, but news of Gerber's savage murder has many locals fearing they are trapped with an escalating endocannibal.

Gerber's remains were discovered around dawn by two Hadenfeldt watchmen dispatched to track him down after he missed his scheduled check-in time. The pair also discovered a bloody trail leading to the Pierce Tomb, but there was no evidence the killer attempted to enter despite a small pool of blood outside the door.

"A fainter trail leading south towards the Lich Street entrance soon petered out," Waldron reports as he paces Armitage's office. "There were no witnesses, no security cameras in the Burying Ground, and what few CCTV cameras there are in the surrounding neighborhoods are all live streaming, so the nut job got clean away. And that has every cop's blood on the boil. Gerber is one of theirs, and he wasn't just eviscerated. He was shredded. I've rarely seen the like in all my years. Whatever ripped into him is an animal. I don't care if it walks upright or not."

Derby asks, "A lycanthrope maybe?"

Waldron blinks. "You're speaking clinically, I hope."

"I am."

"You mean this guy thinks he's a werewolf?" Norton puts in over Skype on Armitage's PC.

"If he does, it could be a connection between Harris House and the Gardner farm."

Armitage: "How so, Edward?"

"According to Elliott's research, the family who owned the land before the Harrises were descendents of Jacques Roulet, a convicted cannibal and lycanthrope."

"That's a bit of a stretch, don't you think?"

Norton: "I don't follow. This virus isn't going to start a zombie apocalypse or something, is it?"

"Don't be facetious," Derby says. "Dr. Whipple is a respected expert on Providence history who lent his expertise to his grand-nephew's research. Even so, Elliott was only able to locate sketchy information about the Roulets, who vanished after living in Providence for a century."

"Probably moved away."

"Certainly a possibility, but Elliott suspected their neighbors murdered the Roulets and buried them on their own property."

Armitage: "Why?"

"Unknown. Again, the information is sketchy. The Roulets were Huguenots who immigrated to New England from Caude. They suffered a good deal of opposition before settling in Providence in 1696, where Etienne Roulet was offered a clerical post by Pardon Tillinghast. Rumor has it that Etienne enjoyed reading 'queer books' and drawing 'queer diagrams' at a time when a hobby like that could get you suspected as a witch. Their son Paul appears to have had an even worse reputation, although Elliott and Whipple were unable to find anything specific about him. Just some wives tales about his prayers 'never being uttered at the proper times or at the proper objects.' Then, around 1730, long after his parents had died, Paul did something awful enough to incite a riot. After that he and the Roulets were never heard from again."

"That doesn't mean Paul was following in Jacques Roulet's footsteps."

Waldron asks what made Elliott suspect Paul and his family lie buried beneath Harris House.

"Logistics. The Harrises employed a servant at one time who insisted the land beneath their home had been used as a burial plot. Elliott was able to locate a lease from 1697 for land the Roulets used to lay out a family graveyard behind their cottage. The land was leased from a home lot granted in 1636 to John Throckmorton, who used an adjoining lot for his family's graveyard. All of the Throckmorton graves were later transferred to the North Burial Ground on Pawtucket West Road when Back Street—which was later renamed Benefit Street—was run through this land, but Elliott was never able to find any records of transference for the Roulet graves, and that's where Harris House stands now."

"Which sounds positively Gothic, but I fail to see -- "

"Something as inexplicable as the Gardner tragedy is going on at Harris House. Can we agree on that? Rather or not the events are directly connected, they do share commonalities. For instance, a disproportionate percentage of Harris House residents have died, and they've done so in a somewhat comparable fashion to the Gardners. Most notably, none of the fatalities displayed any type of anemia or consumption. All just seemed to wither away. True, none of the Harris House fatalities succumbed to symptoms as gruesome the Gardners's gray, brittle death, but they did experience analogous persecution hallucinations about some entity sapping their vitality and willpower."

"All right. Some EB patients have made similar complaints."

"And then there's the vegetation."

Waldron: "What 'vegetation'?"

Norton: "I've got this. Doctors, look at these snaps I took today." Images appear picture-in-picture on the monitor of the Harris House's steep lawn with its early spring growth of insipid grass and weeds. "From what the neighbors tell me, this yard gets weirder looking each year. No, it's not expanding like the blasted heath did, and those creepy looking trees don't sprout fruit, so no one knows if they'd be as inedible as what grew on the Gardner farm. No one's seen any odd-looking wildlife roaming around, either, but maybe that's because there is no wildlife. I didn't spot so much as an old bird's nest or a spider's web, which might also explain why the place seems way too quiet. Anyway, this is nothing compared to what I found in the cellar." The images switch to a video taken with Norton's iPhone of a deep room with brick walls and earthen floor. A huge fireplace with timber lintel—a testament that the cellar once served as a basement kitchen—stands across from the street-side wall. Sunlight filtrates through the grimy glass of two small windows and streams through a thin open doorway. Tree roots thrust through loose foundation stones in several places, twisting in somehow diabolic or quasi-human shapes. None of the contours, however, are as invocative as a cloudy patch of whitish mould or niter redolent of a curled human being on the floor near the fireplace. Squiggly toadstools and Indian pipes carpet the rest of the floor, sprouting thickest near the profile.

The video freezes here. "I don't know if it means anything, but the whole house has a weird reek. Like when someone has a fever. But it's strongest in the cellar."

"Emanating from the fungi?" Armitage asks.

"I couldn't say for sure, but the owner tells me the odor is there even when no fungus is blooming."

Waldron: "You talked to the owner?"

"That's how I got inside. He loaned me a key."

"Trusting fellow."

"Oh, he's okay, especially when you consider he gets journalists as well as history buffs and ghost hunters coming around quite a bit asking about the place. His name's Carrington Harris. Since he can't rent the place, he usually obliges them. That includes Whipple. The doctor talked with Harris a few times over the years. Not in a while, though, and Whipple never asked to go inside. Elliott did, though. He borrowed a key a couple of weeks ago, but Harris had no idea the two were related until I told him."

Armitage: "I suppose Elliott had no reason to mention it."

"It would have made things easier for the police if he had. Elliott didn't return the key the next day as agreed, and Harris had no idea Elliott was a Miskatonic student or lived in Arkham. When he couldn't contact Elliott, he went to the house to make sure it was locked up and found the cellar door open."

"Did he find anything more?"

"Yes. Inside the cellar was a cot, two folding chairs, an LED lantern, and a card table. They all looked new and they were all upended. He also found a shattered Crookes tube."

Armitage repeated: "'Crookes tube'?"

"Whipple owns a collection of antique medical instruments. The police are checking to see if it came from that." Chuckles. "I guess it's better than action figures."

"What purpose would Elliott have for bringing a Crookes tube?"

Derby: "Whatever it was, the tube and the two chairs do suggest that Dr. Whipple accompanied Elliott to the cellar."

"Agreed, but to what end? If Elliott was trying to prove his theory about the Roulets's fate, why not rent a pipe and cable locator or bring along shovels instead of an electrical discharge tube?"

Norton: "Hopefully the police can figure it out. I know they're glad to finally get some sort of lead on Whipple. Oh, by the way, Harris found one more thing." The video starts again. "This was near one of the chairs." A stain or puddle of some green viscous fluid comes into view. "Any idea what this is?"

Armitage: "Looks in some ways like oil."

Norton freezes the video. "Harris called the cops right after I returned his key and told him about Elliott and Whipple, and they had us meet them at the house. I watched SID collect this stuff so they could ID it, and, until they do, the cops are asking me and Harris to keep mum about what we know. I hope you guys are cool with that, because Providence PD has always treated me square."

Armitage, Derby, and Waldron agree before the doctor adds: "CDC called the hospital before I came here, requesting samples of any green viscid matter we found in association with the EB patients."

"Wow. They're not wasting any time."

Derby remembers the lab summary. "Wasn't something like this smeared on the bottom of Elliott's pants?"

Waldron: "There was, but we were never able to establish any link between what was on Elliott's clothes and EB. Maybe CDC will have better luck."

Derby nods and rubs his eyes. "After all this, we're still not any closer."

Waldron disagrees. "All that matters is identifying and quantifying EB so we can fight it, and hopefully we're now on the right track to doing that. If what you two have uncovered helps to solve what happened to Dr. Whipple, so much the better."

Norton: "Thanks, Doc." Snaps his fingers. "Hey! What about your man-eater?"

Waldron shakes his head. "I doubt there's any connection between EB and this cannibal. I just pray that maniac is nabbed before anyone else gets butchered."

7

"The monster's in my grandfather's house!"

It has been a nightmarish night and dispatcher Ken McClure of the Arkham PD is tired and his patience is running low. The caller sounds like a young woman, but her whispering makes it hard to understand her. Sounding harsher than he means to, he asks, "Can you speak up please?"

Still whispering: "It's sleeping in my grandfather's bedroom! There's blood all over the bed and floor! And other things! I don't know how I walked by it!"

"Tell me where you are, ma'am." McClure sits up and waves two patrol officers entering the public-safety answering point, Alfred Morris and Isabel Lewis, over to give them the address.

"Crane Street?" Lewis cheeps as she scrambles into the interceptor utility vehicle.

Morris climbs in on the driver's side. "I know. That's where we found the first body, that suicide." As he pulls away from the station, no lights or sirens, "Call all units to meet us there, silent run."

In the PSAP, McClure asks the caller her name.

"Georgina Kalem."

"Hi, Georgina. Listen, patrol cars are on their way. They will be there in less than two minutes. Can you get out of the house?"

"No!" Kalem is in a bedroom in a rear corner of the house, a full Cape Cod built in the eighteenth century. Backtracking to the front door means passing through the keeping room (a combination kitchen/living/family room) and past the master bedroom where the gory squatter lays sprawled. The back door is positioned directly in front of the master bedroom's open doorway, and, to complicate matters, has a sheet of clear plastic insulation tacked over it from winter.

"Can you go out a window?"

"There's only one and it's warped! He'd hear me open it!"

Lewis radios in that she and Morris are 10-23 (arrived at scene) along with three more patrol cars.

"That's okay. Listen, Georgina, officers are outside and will be coming in soon, so I want you to find a place to hide. Can you do that?"

"Yes." Kalem crouches behind a wardrobe.

"Good. Now stay on the phone with me, but keep quiet until you hear the officers are inside and shout 'clear.' Can you do that?"

"Yes."

"That's good. You're doing great, Georgina."

"Uh-huh." For a few moments the only sound is Kalem's exhilarated breathing, then: "I took a video of whoever it is. Sleeping. If that can help you."

You did what? Stifling his bewilderment, McClure says, "Thank you, Georgina, but right now I need you to keep hiding and stay on the phone with me. Okay?"

"Okay."

McClure listens to the officers coordinate. An instant's fatigue creeps through his adrenalin surge, so he swallows some dark coffee for a recharge. He and every sworn personnel have been on the go since sunset and woefully behind as the cannibal not only escalated but blossomed into a full-blown demon.

Eight home invasions.

Fourteen men, women, and children dead.

Any bodies not devoured were maimed into shapeless remnants.

A feeble waxing crescent moon did not help the search. Did streetlights show glimmers of the killer or conceal the monster? The few witnesses were not very helpful, their descriptions weirdly abstract. Condensed, the cannibal seemed to resemble either a malformed ape or anthropomorphic fiend.

"Try getting a sketch artist to put that on paper," one frustrated detective grumbled. "Only in a college town."

Sunrise brought a cessation of the carnage, and by eight o'clock the berserker had apparently gone to ground.

"I was looking for his annuity," Kalem whispers.

"Don't talk," McClure reflexively instructs.

Kalem cannot stop herself. "Grandfather told me he has an annuity with a death benefit before he …" Swallows. "It wasn't in his deposit box. I thought -- "

"Stop talking, Georgina. *Now.*"

A few moments silence, then: "I hear something."

"The officers are getting ready to enter. Did you leave the front door unlocked?"

Kalem has to think, it seems so long ago. "Yes."

"Good. After they come inside, where do they go?"

"Down the hall. Turn left past the stairway. It's the first door on the left."

"All right. Now hunker down. Here we go."

The next twelve seconds are the longest in McClure's life as his imagination interprets what he hears like a kid listening to *Lights Out* on the radio.

A distant door gradually opens.

Soft padding of several footsteps comes closer.

Halts.

Violence erupts.

Shouting.

A roar. Nothing human about it.

Screaming. A familiar voice. Lewis?

One gunshot.

Another roar, searing with anguish.

Morris: "He's down!"

More scuffling as the perpetrator is subdued.

A new voice: "Clear!"

Lewis: "Oh God! Oh my God!"

McClure tells Kalem: "Don't move! Shout so the officers can find you!"

Kalem shouts.

Soon Detective Ted Allison is on the phone. "We can stand down."

"Lewis? Is she hurt?"

"The lunatic bit her! Ripped a chunk right out of her leg like a shark! EMTs are on their way."

"Who shot who?"

"Morris shot the crazy in the ribs. Kind of a lucky shot, this creep moves so fast."

Later McClure hears how the cannibal was taken to St. Mary's, where the crazy had to be sedated with a far higher dosage than the average agitated adult perpetrator. How it was impossible to describe much about the cannibal until after clean up and how awful it was discovering the cannibal's identity.

"None of us could believe it," Allison tells McClure. "Maybe the docs at Mass Hospital can figure out what happened. Even with the quarantine, the powers-that-be think MH is best qualified to handle this. I can tell you right now, though, this is never going to make any sense."

* * *

8

Allan Halsey is arriving.

Tranquilized and trussed, the Dean is transported to a behavioral assessment room in the crisis stabilization ward where he is put under Barnard's care. After reading Halsey's medical report, Barnard calls Halsey's physician. "If anyone else had signed off on this, Doc, I'd demand an inquiry."

Waldron sighs. "I almost called for one myself, but our best attending physician did the admission history and physical assessment."

"Allan's blood pressure, CBC and BMP results, the EKG and EEG readings -- "

"They're off the charts."

"His heart is fibrillating and his pulse is erratic."

"It's like Allan's red-lining with his transmission stuck in second gear."

"Well, the term 'short-circuiting' is what came to my mind."

"I can't understand why his body hasn't given out before now. Even a broken ankle didn't slow him down. This is inconceivable!"

"It is difficult to associate Allan with the atrocities, but I see the blood on his clothes and the viscera he had with him when he was apprehended match up with the various victims. When the DNA results of skin samples collected from under the victims's fingernails come in, I'll be stunned if they don't match with Allan." Barnard sighs. "I might have to assign his psyche assessment to another psychiatrist. This one is hitting too close to home. I can't even begin to imagine what could have caused his breakdown."

"I felt the same way, Harold, but who else can you bring in? There isn't a doctor in New England who doesn't know and respect Allan. Listen, our best neurologists are checking to see if any type of seizure affected Allan's amygdale, hypothalamus, or even his anterior cingulated cortex. Something made Allan drive into that stop sign and abandon his car. I'll email you their findings as soon as I have them."

"Well, a traumatic brain injury can cause personality changes. I've seen it all too often in combat soldiers. However, Allan's accident didn't appear to be violent. Not much more than a fender bender. Still, if he wasn't wearing his seatbelt and he banged his head against the steering wheel, the force of the impact could have been focused on the area of his prefrontal cortex."

"Sounds like you're already starting to work the problem."

"Don't give me too much credit. We might never learn what happened to him."

"We'll certainly never know if we don't try, and I aim to try. Before I forget, though, I'm sorry about all the handling problems getting Allan to you."

"No need to apologize. The hassles were all on your end. Allan's isolated and we'll follow established quarantine protocol until Arkham is in the clear. Hopefully that's soon. I also think your suspicions are right and EB had nothing to do with Allan's collapse. I can't recall of an isolated case like Allan's being triggered by a virus."

Waldron and Barnard talk for a few more minutes before disconnecting. In the Miskatonic Student Services Building, Waldron prepares to return to St. Mary's when a student knocks on his door. "Yes? Dr. West, isn't it?"

"Yes, sir. I didn't want to interrupt while you were speaking on the phone, but I just heard about Dr. Halsey. I'm afraid we had a difference of opinion the last time I saw him."

"Did you?"

"Over the best course of treatment for EB patients."

"I see. Well, you're hardly the only one who disagreed with Dr. Halsey about that."

"I still wish it hadn't happened. Has there been any further word on his condition?"

"I'm afraid not. Don't spread it around, but I don't think I'm violating confidentiality if I tell you we have no idea what his condition is. He's getting excellent care, though, and if anything can be done for him I promise you it will be."

"I see. Thank you."

Waldron locks his office. "I'm heading back to the hospital. You can talk with me more on the way if you like."

"That's kind of you."

"And don't worry about your disagreement. Dr. Halsey never held a grudge in his life, nor did he expect his students to always agree with him. If you feel like you need to make anything up to him, concentrate on your patients. That's all any of us can do, at least until the quarantine is lifted."

"Do you think I'd be allowed to visit him after that?"

"I couldn't say. Dr. Barnard's is handling Dr. Halsey's case. Give him a call and feel free to mention my name."

"I appreciate that, Dr. Waldron. More than you can know.

9

"Randolph Carter is ready to leave."

Carter does not know how to react. "Are you sure?"

Barnard pats Carter's shoulder. "I know it can be jarring to hear this, but we need your bed for someone who needs it more than you."

"I see."

"You don't sound happy."

"I'm relieved. And confused. I can't return to Arkham right now."

"No, but the quarantine will eventually be lifted."

"Hotels can be expensive, and, remember, I lost my job."

"Isn't there anyone you can stay with?"

"All my friends live in Arkham."

"No one in your hometown?"

"Some family. All cousins, most of them distant. I'd prefer not going there so soon after this."

Instead of pressing that Carter had nothing to be ashamed of, Barnard nods. "How about Providence?"

A name comes to mind. "There might be someone. We were dormmates as undergrads. He's more a friend of a friend now. Can I use my phone?"

Carter speed dials Derby, who conferences Norton, who is happy to let Carter bunk on his foldout couch. "No one told me you were in the hospital. Man, I'm sorry. I would have come see you."

"That's all right. Edward can tell you I wouldn't have been very good company."

"Better than most of my dates lately, I bet. Hey, maybe you can help with a story we're working on while you're here."

Derby: "That's an excellent idea!"

Carter is intrigued. "You two are collaborating?"

Norton: "I suppose you could say that. We can't talk about it on the phone, though, and you'll have to keep it hush-hush for now. What do you say I pick you up tomorrow after you're discharged and give you the back-story on the drive home?"

"I appreciate that, but the hospital has a shuttle to Providence and there's something I want to do when I get there. I can call you when I'm finished, if that's all right."

It is, which leaves Carter with one last person to inform.

After lights out, Carter waits for another exposition of sleep to come upon him. Dozing off, he wakes around four and realizes he did not dream. Feeling sideways, he abandons his room, and, avoiding the night staff, slips into Slaader's room.

Carter gasps.

He hasn't seen Slaader since the night of his dream, and his mentor is so emaciated that his restraints are gone, replaced by IVs and wires leading to a heart monitor.

"Joe?" Carter edges closer, like a child approaching an open casket at his first funeral as Slaader's eyes follow him. "Joe? Are you all right?"

The answer reverberates in Carter's head: *"Joe Slaader is dead."*

"Call him my host."

CHAPTER FOUR

HORRORS BEYOND HORRORS

1

Randolph Carter is sitting on a dilapidated tomb.

That is where Norton finds his friend in Providence's North Burial Ground, per Carter's directions. Carter is wearing what looks like the same brown two-piece he wore to Honors Program confabs and Debating Union meetings, along with the same matching snap brim fedora cocked on his head. A well-traveled black carry-on leans against the tomb. "What ho! Why on earth did you want to meet here?"

A grin flutters over Carter's lips, but his eyes never brighten. "I wanted to visit my parents."

"Uhhh … you're not sitting on …?"

'Heavens no." Carter waves behind Norton. "They're over there."

"Oh."

"This just seemed like a pleasant spot to wait."

The pleasant spot is in the North Burial Ground's oldest section and filled with simple greenstone markers and slate stones carved with the usual death's heads, hourglasses, and coffins. As for the tomb Carter is sitting on, the names, dates, and most of the inscriptions are worn away, but Norton can still make out the epitaph:

> Husband and wife did twelve children bear,
> Dy'd the same day; alike both aged were
> Both eighty years they liv'd, Five hours did part
> (Ev'n on the marriage day) Each tender heart
> So fit a match, surely could never be;
> Both in their lives, and in their deaths agree.

Jabbing a thumb towards the tomb: "That almost sounds like a riddle."

"It wouldn't stupefy me if it were."

Norton nods. "You ready to take off?"

"Can you spare me one more minute? It's nice being outside again."

"Sure." Shrugs. "Of course, if you wanted, we could go to Blackstone Park. Watch the Seekonk. That's where I go to relax."

"Thanks, but this is fine."

"Yeah, okay." Norton clears his throat.

"Is something wrong?"

Twitches. Lowers his voice: "It's just … see … I don't do death."

Carter smirks. "Pardon?"

"You heard me."

"I did, but I'm having trouble understanding you."

"I don't like funerals. So I don't go. Which means I try to avoid graveyards as much as possible."

"I see." Muses on that. "You know, graveyards are more than a depository for the dead. There were some Greek philosophers who frequented cemeteries to take advantage of the solitude to contemplate and write."

"Why am I not surprised you know something like that?"

"I don't see where that's worse than ignoring that people die."

"Don't put words in my mouth, Carter. What the deuce is it to me if they do, anyway?"

"Death is omnipresent. Inevitable. How can you pretend it doesn't exist?"

"You just do and it doesn't. *Viola!*"

"That's puerile."

"So says the man in the Indiana Jones hat."

"A touchstone to a more preferable time." Carter beams, this time with his whole face. "All right, *touché*. And truce. You are my host, and I am your guest, so I'll change the subject. Now that we're alone, so to speak, how can I help with this story you and Derby are working on?"

Norton swings a finger like a metronome and simpers, "I'm glad you brought that up."

2

"Harley Warren is on TV?"

Norton is more bemused than surprised as Carter watches the braggadocios professor on his 85" HD television.

"Yes," Carter mutters, scrutinizing the interview from the convertible sofa, copies of Elliott's Harris House research as well as Derby and Norton's spread out on the cushions and floor around him.

"What channel?"

"AJE."

"*The Stream?*"

"Yes."

"Weird place for him to show up."

Warren is looking tan, rested, and ready somewhere near Haradh in Al-Hasa as he chats about searching for Irem of the Pillars. "Like Juris Zarins, I associate Irem with Ubar, so I'm seeking a geographic region and a specific people, not merely a specific city."

Carter: "Oh, you're looking for a city, all right."

The interviewer points out that people have been searching for the Atlantis of the deserts practically since Allah drove King Shaddad and his people into the sands for defying the prophet Hud's warnings against their occult worship of stone idols. "What makes you think you'll be the one to locate it?"

Warren smiles into the camera and Carter shivers, convinced Warren is aware that he is watching. "All I'll say about that for now is that I recently uncovered something truly wonderful that should lead the way to ultimate success."

Norton guffaws. "Still the same blowhard."

Carter remembers: *"Harley Warren is dead."* Then mumbles: "He may not be the same person you remember."

Ten bucks says any changes haven't been for the better." As the interview concludes, Norton asks, "So you think he's wrong? Irem is a city?"

"What I think is Warren isn't looking for Irem. He's only saying that to get to the official permissions and clearances he needs to search for The Nameless City."

"What nameless city?"

"A city that is supposedly older than mankind."

"You mean prehistoric? Like Ponape?"

"No, I mean primordial, like Neoproterozoic."

"That's creepy. What makes you think Warren's running a ruse?"

"Because I got a glimpse of the 'truly wonderful' item he uncovered when we were in Florida. At least I think I did." Carter trembles. *"Harley Warren is dead."* "Anyway, it doesn't matter at this moment."

Norton's smart phone starts spouting the Derek Flint ringtone. "Excuse me. That's my private line." He walks away to take the call as Carter stands to stretch and give the Pearl Street loft another sour evaluation. Norton notices before answering. "I knew you wouldn't like it here."

"I like it fine."

"But this place isn't to your tastes."

"It's just stone, brick, and mortar."

Actually, the twilight view of Providence from the third floor of the refurbished nineteenth century brass hinge factory is spectacular. It is the inside that Carter finds unappealing. He adores the post and beam construction and restored brick walls and wooden floors, but abhors the neutral-painted gypsum walls, blonde European kitchen cabinetry, and stainless steel and glass railing on the diamond plate stairway. As he walks to a window to watch more and more stars sparkle in the darkening sky, he remembers, *"Joe Slaader is dead."* Then, more to himself than Norton, "For what it's worth, I learned more in the past couple of weeks than I ever could have from Warren. About myself and many other things. Learning is just memory, though. It's not the same as knowledge. To know requires application and belief in yourself."

Norton disconnects, grabs a notepad, and jots. "That was one of my confidential sources in the PD, and he just passed along some very interesting news. As we speak the Department of Public Works is approving plans to excavate Benefit Street in front of Harris House starting tomorrow morning. The official reason is to repair a crumbling sewer pipe."

"But your informant thinks they might be looking for a nameless city instead?"

"He doesn't think, roomy, he knows. Public Works has been replacing the city's original clay sewer pipes the past few years, but they use this thing called trenchless cured-in-place pipe lining as a time and money saver. Digging is strictly for emergencies like a busted main. When my CS got wind of the rush being put on this excavation, he did some snooping and found out SID identified human DNA in that green goop from the cellar. A bunch of different DNA, most of which aren't on any database."

Carter scrounges for a page from Elliott and Whipple's research. "So Elliott may have been correct about the house being built over the Roulet family plot. That's most likely their DNA."

"That's one reason for the cover story. Can you imagine the zoo that will swamp Benefit Street if it gets out the City is removing human remains from under the house?"

"I can. What's the other reason?"

"To prevent an even bigger zoo if news gets out SID was able to identify Whipple's DNA is in that goop."

Carter claps his hands and shouts, "Finally, something makes sense!"

"Excuse me? Whipple bite you when you were a child?"

"What?"

"You sound happy he may be dead."

"Who? Whipple? I didn't mean that at all." Carter finds the paper and hands it to Norton before he begins searching the Internet on his smart phone. "Here. This is a copy of the lease the Roulets signed for their family plot."

"Okay."

"Did you read it?"

"I tried."

"I'll give you that. Secretary hand takes getting used to. According to a marginalia, the leased lot was a 'damned patch' where 'only aberrancy sprouts.'"

"Sounds like the Harris House lawn."

"It does, doesn't it? From what I understand it's also a good description of the blasted heath, but this lease is from the seventeen century."

"Oh, I get you. The Gardner tragedy and Harris House can't be connected because the meteor didn't arrive until the twentieth century."

"So our current understanding of Time and Space would have us believe, but their similarities still intrigue me. And that Crookes tube ..." Stops searching and begins reading.

"What about the Crookes tube?"

"They have a limited number of uses. I remember Professor Reed using a modern rotating anode ray tube in his physics class, but Whipple probably didn't have one of those in his collection, so he grabbed what was at hand."

"You are going to tell me something that makes sense soon. Right?"

"Afraid not." Carter consults his Timex wristwatch. "That excavation doesn't leave me time right now to explain further. I need to dash to Brown University. Would you be a lamb and run an errand that requires a bit of driving."

"I suppose. Where to?"

"Seabrook, New Hampshire."

"You call that a little driving?"

"It has the nearest stores I can find that sell fireworks."

"Why do you need fireworks? It's April!"

"I'm in desperate need of something loud and powerful like an M-80. Purchase two dozen of them, just to be safe. If they don't sell M-80s, get the biggest salutes you're permitted to purchase." Holds up his smart phone to show Norton a map. "See? It's near the border."

"I don't care if it's down the block! I'm not going anywhere until you tell me why you think you need two dozen baby dynamite sticks!"

"Because some concussive force might come in handy later, and this is the best way that I can think of on the spur of the moment to procure them." Carter looks every which way. "Did you see where I put my hat?"

3

Richard Upton Pickman is sketching something weird.

Which is nothing new, but this time is different.

Pickman, like Bansky, believes art should comfort the disturbed or disturb the comfortable, so he usually only feels satisfied when his paintings get on people's nerves or harrow up someone's imagination. Since returning from Cold Island, however, memories of his fraught excursion have crouched within a hand's reach of his thoughts. Unable to flee to the succor of Fort Point or Red Hook, and confident in his art's ability to lay bare any person or place's soul, Pickman decides to confront his agitation by investigating Keziah Mason's room while Gilman is risking a second river jaunt.

Gaining Banaczek's permission to sketch the garret gable under pretense of surprising Gilman with a painting of his new apartment, it does not take long for Pickman to realize the good size room is as off as Cold Island. Corners do not match up precisely, doors are not exactly square, and the north wall slants inward so much that a disproportional cavity must exist between it and in back of the boarded up window of the plumbed outer wall. The low ceiling similarly slants in this direction, but all these irregularities are noticeable, especially since Pickman's senses seem to have grown incrementally sharper since entering the room, and what Pickman finds himself worrying most about is unperceivable. Something in the room's angles suggest a hidden design beyond his abilities to discern except in a deep, primal part of his brain. A frustrating observation made manifest after Pickman leaves for The White Ship, where he realizes some sort of macropsia caused him to draw both a rat hole in the north wall's baseboard and the level loft above the attic much too large, gross errors Gilman delights in when Pickman lays out the sketch on the bar for him and Elton. "I've heard of blind spots, R.U., but I think you embedded your submanifolds a tad much."

"Laugh while you can, monkey boy." Pickman's rejoinder only makes Gilman laugh harder. "I don't know why those areas came out the way they did, but the rest of the room is representational, as you well know."

Elton looks up from the sketch to ask Gilman. "What were you saying about Dr. Caligari?"

Gilman's face blanks. "Huh?"

"Don't ya remember? Ya were wondering who'd want to build a room like this." Elton asks Pickman, "Any idea why ya supersized the open rat hole but none of the stopped up ones?"

Pickman peers at the sketch. "I don't know. I don't even remember drawing any rat holes." Takes a closer look. "Or that." Points to an aperture in the level loft that appears to have long ago been swathed with mortised planking secured with wooden pegs. "Has anyone heard where EB causes fugue states?"

"Ya don't look ill to me."

"So then what's going on?" Pickman scratches his forehead with the fingers of both hands. "Maybe I'm suffering from a fervor instead of a fever."

"Why's that?"

"The whole time I was sketching, I felt this gnawing in my mind. It was like I could sense something intrinsic about the room's dimensions, but I couldn't figure out what it is."

"Now you're sounding like Walter with his obsession."

Gilman raps the bar. "Yeah, you do. Great minds must think alike because the first time I stepped into Mason' room, something about it got under my skin, too. I even told Basil I was thinking about asking you to look so I could get your perspective on its perspectives."

"Why didn't you?"

"Because Derby sidetracked me with Cold Island first. Not that that excuses you for sneaking into my room like you did. Since you did, though, don't you think its perspectives are off?"

"You can see for yourself they're queerly unbalanced." Pickman scowls as he pores over the sketch.

Elton: "What exactly is unbalanced about them?"

"Perspective is a method of organizing forms in space. Artists primarily use it to create the illusion of depth or space on a two-dimensional surface. Here, the various axes don't properly converge at their point of perspective."

Gilman: "They're off."

"You like saying that, don't you?" Pores harder. Scowls harder. "Something about seeing the room this size ... opposed to being surrounded by it ... presents a new perspective on its proportions." Drums a Devil's tattoo with his left hand, then notices something and murmurs, "Leonardo?"

"Don't tell me you see Da Vinci in there."

"In a way." Pickman maneuvers his hands this way and that over the sketch, as if dissecting it or measuring differently-spaced divisions within it. "The innate or conditioned sense of proportions humans possess causes them to regard anything disproportional as ugly or ludicrous."

Elton: "Like Mason's room?"

Pickman either ignores or does not hear him. "The ancient Greeks defined beauty to be correct proportions. For a long time Polykleitos's *Doryphoros* was their exemplar of correct human proportion, but Leonardo Da Vinci took things a step further. His *Vitruvian Man* not only illustrates the ideal body proportions described in Vitruvius's *De architectura*, it demonstrates Leonardo's belief that the workings of human anatomy are an analogy of the workings of the universe."

"Sort of makes you want to treat the average bloke with a little more respect, don't it?"

"Yes, well Leonardo found proportions in everything, from sounds to weights to intervals of time to every active force in existence." Pickman's hands cease as he shakes his head. "I'm not sure how else to say it, Walter. This room is unprecedented."

Gilman asks, "How so?"

"I wish I knew. It's there. I know it's there. I sense it, but I can't isolate it. It's holistic somehow. Maybe Leonardo could isolate it or break it down. He was the polymath's polymath."

"At least elaborate on what you're sensing."

Pickman is stumped for several seconds, but then, "Leonardo uses the power of geometry in his artwork to suggest the inherent order of creation. The best example is *The Last Supper*." Bringing up the painting on his smart phone, Pickman points to the following areas: "The mural itself is six by twelve units in dimension, the back wall is equal to four units, the windows three units, and the recession of the tapestries as widths on the mural's surface is 12:6:4:3."

"I've read about that. Those are the harmonic proportions of music."

"Yes, where 3:4 equals the interval of a fourth, 4:6 the fifth, and 6:12 the octave. Leonardo considered music to be the 'sister of painting' and expounded on the resonances between visual and audio harmonies. He was hoping to find an omnipresent measure: a law in which the phenomena of optical science are measurable, comparable to the musical intervals conceived in his era as the ordering principles of a creation based on number and proportion. To borrow Wallace Stevens, he had what you could call a blessed rage for order."

"I've read about that, too. What does any of it have to do with Mason's room?"

"Leonardo was just as passionate about ultimate disorder and cataclysmic destruction, especially as he grew older. His deluge drawings are prime examples of this." Pickman brings up one of the drawings. "Now, I'm sure you've also read how, during the Italian Renaissance, the circle was considered the image of divine perfection, the five Platonic solids the building blocks of the cosmos, and the human figure the microcosm of the universe. I refer you again to *Vitruvian Man*, whose extensions are encompassed by the circumscribed shapes of the circle and the square. However, Leonardo also understood how *fortuna* stands against *virtú*; how the blind hand of fate can frustrate our best-laid plans, no matter how efficaciously or excellently carried out." Pickman traces the index finger of his left hand around the sketch. "Mason's room here suggests something more menacing than *fortuna* I think. I can't pinpoint any harmonic proportions within it, rather it's 12:6:4:3 or the Golden Ratio. This room is the essence of disproportional." Pickman's finger rounds the sketch over and over, like a planetoid caught in a non-elliptical orbit. "For most of his life, Leonardo concentrated on the perfection of the circle and geometric forms allied to it as the generating forms of the house of God. When I first saw Mason's room it looked square; but, the longer I looked, the more it strikes me as being a circle. A not-quite-perfect circle with an image that has nothing to do with the divine." Stops tracing and taps the oversized open rat hole and sealed aperture. "That's the best I can describe it, anyway. Like I said, it's unprecedented."

Several seconds pass before Elton stares at Gilman.

Gilman stares back. "What?"

"Just thinking."

"Thinking what?"

"Maybe ya should stop asking who would build a room like this and start asking why anyone would want anything to do with a place like that."

* * *

4

"Aldin Norton is losing his patience."

Carter waits for a long exhale before asking Norton, "Any particular reason why you're referring to yourself in the third person?"

"Because Aldin Norton is worried! Okay? The cops will throw us in the can for breaking and entering if we get caught!"

"Go home then. I'll let you know if I find anything."

"Forgive me, but, as mysterious as you're acting, I think I'll stay. You owe me a story after the loan of my sofa and running me to New Hampshire."

"All right, but remaining is your choice."

The men are squatting behind a thicket near the top of the steep rise along the east side of Harris House. After burrowing and then stripping some of the rotted clapboards off the home, they bore through the exposed planking and insulation. Once inside the vast, raftered attic, they weave through chests, chairs, and spinning-wheels to a ladder descending to the third floor, where they make their way along corridors of peeling wallpaper and falling plaster, past rooms cluttered with battered remnants of abandoned furniture, and down rickety staircases until reaching the dank, humid cellar.

"That's some peculiar odor," Carter remarks. "I thought I noticed it upstairs, but it's definite here."

"Like someone smells when they're sick. At least we can see a little better now," thanks to the luminescent fungi blanketing the floor except where the oddly anthropomorphic niter patch lies near the fireplace. On their way to Harris House, Carter had Norton stop at a big box store so they could purchase a pair of bazaar folding chairs and a battery-powered toaster. Norton unfolds the chairs, unpacks the toaster from its box, and pulls out a paper sack of M-80s from his coat pocket before sitting down to wait. For what, though, he is not sure, so Norton inquires once more, but Carter requests, "Please test the toaster to make sure it works."

"We did that already."

"Humor me." Carter sets a hard-sided instrument carrying case that could pass for a large tackle box on the ground.

"Coils fire right up, just like in the store and on the drive here."

Carter snaps the case's latches open.

"Look, if this could get dangerous, don't you think I have a right to know?"

"Of course it could be dangerous. That's why I wanted the salutes. And I told you that you could go home."

"And I said I'm staying."

"Then you do so at your own risk and I owe you zilch." Carter slides the housing for an anode tube insert out of the carrying case, places it on the ground beside his chair, and tests it. "All charged up and ready to rock."

"Did Reed loan that to you?"

"Hardly. He's passed away. An acquaintance in Brown's Physics Department that owed me a favor let me borrow it. You remember Brent Truax?"

"Why would I remember him?"

"He was your natural science tutor."

"Oh. Right. Brent Truax. Nice guy." Lets a moment pass. "He must be to let you borrow that. Looks pricy."

"Nothing any decent muckraker's annual salary can't cover if we break it."

Norton blows a Bronx cheer. "You break it, you bought it. So this is the state-of-the-art counterpart of Whipple's cathode ray tube?"

"Close enough for government work."

"What sort of work would that be? Whipple brought his ray tube here for a reason. What do you think that is?"

"Let's see if we can find out." Carter switches on the ray tube, dousing the cellar in a blue light. "The way I understand it, a cathode ray tube is really only good for projecting electrons or demonstrating magnetic deflection in electrons. My guess is Whipple must have been trying to detect an otherwise imperceptible force he suspected exists here. Otherwise he must have wanted to shoot a stream of ether radiation at something."

"I'll worry about what ether radiation is later and ask what he would want to shoot it at."

"Whatever tenacious malignancy he suspected might be responsible for the disproportionate number of wasting deaths in Harris House."

"You mean like radiation treatment on cancer? My dad had that."

"I remember, and, yes, I suppose something like that." Carter waits another minute before switching off the ray tube. "Nothing." He sits and consults his Timex. "When do they begin excavating?"

"Around six."

"It's nearly midnight now. If nothing happens by five we better cut out, in case the crew arrives early. Best we leave the same way we entered."

"Works for me." Norton sits and zips his coat shut. "This place gives me the creeps."

"It's just stone, brick, and mortar."

Another Bronx cheer. "So's the Amityville house." Draws his collar closer around his neck. "So what do you think happened to Whipple? For real. It's obvious you read more in what Derby sent me than I did."

"You read everything I did. I fancy I may have had the opportunity to be able to deduce a little more."

"Like what? I don't care if it's *outré*. I know a little something about the willing suspension of disbelief."

"Except this is real life, not fiction, and I've apparently had trouble differentiating lately between where madness ends and reality begins. Maybe that's all this is."

"You mean madness? Better not be. Not after a tank of gas and eight bucks for fireworks." Norton pats Carter's shoulder. "Whatever your theory is, it can't be any more nonlinear than that coroner's report about the Gardner family."

"If memory serves, no one took Aylesworth seriously."

"I wasn't saying he couldn't have been right. I was just trying to make a point. Look, our science writer, Kyle Garrett, wrote a really insightful article on panspermia just last year. I'm well aware that there's more in Heaven and Earth and all that, so I'm not going to throw shade at you, if that's what you're worried about."

Carter squirms in his seat, more to brace himself than to get comfortable. "Fine." Deep breath. What was the best way to dissect this intrusion of the irrational? "Do you believe in vampires, little boy?"

Norton frowns, feigning concentration. *All right, then.* An experienced enough interviewer to know Carter will clam up if he makes a crack, he asks back, "Why vampires?"

"I asked you first."

"You did, but Whipple's DNA wasn't found in a pool of blood. Besides, if you really thought there was a chance of running into Janos Skorzeny tonight, why doesn't your arsenal include a cross, a stake, and a mallet?"

"I might have erred there; but, like you say, there was no blood. There are different kinds of vampires, however, not all of whom feast on blood. For instance, in some areas of Russia they believe a vampire remains in its grave where it chews on his feet and hands until—one by one—its relatives sicken and die. Which sounds a little like what's been happening here." Nervous pause. "It also sounds crazy."

"It might if I hadn't seen that green goop and didn't know what was in it, or we were in my apartment during the middle of the day instead of here at midnight by the light of these glowing 'shrooms. So tell me more."

"All right. Just remember, you asked."

"Yes, I did."

"Have you heard of the New England Vampire Panic?"

"The sequel to the Salem witch trials? Sure."

"Every year more cases are being documented of bodies having been exhumed and 'treated' as *nosferatu* throughout backwoods New England during the 1800s. Henry David Thoreau even commented on the practice, and the Smithsonian recently published a really insightful article about the panic."

Norton scrunches his nose. "I was being sincere about Garrett's article, and I've read about some of those exhumations. That kind of thing makes news, so I know they always coincided with an outbreak of tuberculosis. The yokels were confusing its symptoms with vampire attacks."

"What if there was more to it than just tuberculosis?"

"Such as?"

"Thoreau as well as several contemporary newspaper articles blamed the migration of rural Rhode Islanders into Vermont and Connecticut for spreading the practice of digging up suspected corpses to cut off their heads and burning their hearts and lungs. What nobody knows is when this practice started. Manias rarely spring up overnight. The origin of the Salem witch trials is rooted in earlier witch trials in Europe." Carter takes another deep breath. "Let's suppose word reaches Providence that Paul's ancestor had been sentenced as a werewolf in Touraine. France was going through a Werewolf Panic at the time, so I doubt Jacques was a shape-shifter, but he was a cannibal. Now mix in Etienne's peculiar taste in books and his penchant for drawing peculiar diagrams, and then add Paul's dubious reputation. If people in areas like the Nooseneck Hill country are already desecrating suspected corpses, what would it take to spur an otherwise religiously-tolerant community into believing they have Huguenot monsters living in their midst?"

Norton ponders Carter's words, then, "I still don't get what any of this has to do with Whipple, but … if Paul inherited Jacques's taste for human meat, I could see where that would cause an uproar."

"I concur, however I did some research while you were away and couldn't find one case of anything resembling cannibalism or tuberculosis in or around Providence during the early eighteenth century."

"That doesn't prove anything. The mob would have buried any evidence of that with their victims. Sometimes the lack of evidence can be telling."

"So the mystery of what happened to Paul Roulet and his family could end there, but … what if Paul's taste ran more along the lines of those Russian vampires?" Carter proceeds tentatively. "Tuberculosis is a wasting disease, and we know that several people who lived in Harris House over the years succumbed to an inexorable weakness as they wasted away. We also know that some of them described having their breath sucked at night, while others complained of a glassy-eyed, half-visible presence that bit and chewed on them. There was also that servant—Ann White from Kent County—who refused to enter this cellar because she insisted this ground had been used for burial purposes and that a vampire interred here was responsible for the illnesses."

"I remember Elliott mentioning White in his notes, but I must have glossed over the rest."

"Because it sounds crazy?"

Norton grimaces. "Will you stop going there? I'm aware Harley Warren schooled you in parapsychology as well as psychology, so you ought to know there's nothing nutty about thinking White knew what happened to Paul and his family."

"It's hard to say if she did. New England is littered with unmarked family plots. White's insistence about a burial ground could have been nothing more than a lucky guess. That doesn't mean we should gloss over how EB victims exhibit similar symptoms, nor how the Gardner family also succumbed to some sort of virulent wasting disease accompanied by a remorseless enervation bordering on loss of will. We also shouldn't ignore the similarities you noted yourself between the yard outside and the blasted heath. Not only the mutations, but there were several eyewitness reports of an analogous radiance to these mushrooms that seemed to inhere to the vegetation, grass, leaves, and blossoms in and around the Gardner farm."

"Fine, but the blasted heath was expanding, and the Harris House lawn never has."

"Maybe it's never had to. Animals like snapping turtles are content to spend their lives in one spot so long as a steady food supply keeps coming to them." Carter props his elbows on his armrests and steeples his fingers together. "Differences can be as revealing as commonalities. For instance, more than one person suffering the throes of feverish hallucinations in this house was documented to have shouted in a course and idiomatic form of French for hours on end, even though none of them knew more than the rudiments of the language. Xenolalia wasn't reported with the Gardners or been reported with any EB victim, but perhaps that's because those stricken in Harris House were babbling in a language the Roulets were fluent in."

"Wait a second."

"Yes?"

Norton realizes he does not know what more to say

"Here's another for instance. Derby and I have a post-grad friend taking Advanced Mathematics courses at MU. His name's Walter Gilman. He's brilliant, if a bit of a horndog. Gilman's concentration is Multi-Dimensional Reality in Folklore, and, as part of his research, he's living in Keziah Mason's room in Arkham's Witch House starting next Fall."

Norton was tempted to ask why, but waits.

"Now, before I quit working for Warren, we were researching an ancient grimoire called *Al Azif*. I suffered some terrible dreams while working on it. Dreams I feel were partially inspired by abstract formulae within the book. Formulae that can supposedly link our universe's reality with other dimensions. Formulae that continue to flummox today's brightest minds, yet Gilman believes Mason was able to grasp them."

"Sounds intriguing."

"It seems Warren thought so, too. Our *Al Azif* research is likely why he is in Saudi Arabia. Now … what if Etienne and Paul found *Al Azif*—or a translation of it known as the *Necronomicon*—intriguing, too? It would definitely qualify as a queer book, and Etienne's penchant for drawing queer diagrams might have been his attempts to work out those formulae. Paul reportedly wasn't much for book learning, so I suspect his grasp of the material was more intuitive." Carter shrugs. "If Mason is any indication, some people have an affinity for it." Adjusts in his chair. "I can't tell you yet if or how all this ties in with Whipple, but I do know that the man who wrote *Al Azif*—Abdul Alhazred—paid a price for his efforts. Several witnesses in a Samarran marketplace watched something unseen drain Alhazred's life-force until his body collapsed into gray ash." Bores eyes into Norton. "Not exactly the same as a pool of putrescent, I know, but doesn't any of that sound familiar? Or is it just my imagination?"

5

Randolph Carter is alone with his thoughts.

"Harley Warren is dead."

"Joe Slaader is dead."

The words run rings from the back to the front of his mind and around again.

"Joe Slaader is dead."

"Harley Warren is dead."

It is almost three o'clock and Norton is sleeping.

"Harley Warren is dead."

"Joe Slaader is dead."

Carter keeps watch over his companion after having nodded off himself about an hour ago and suffering his first nightmare since meeting Slaader.

There was no Warren or Nyarlathotep or Miskatonic University or haunted Arkham or blasphemous city with its champing and boundless demon-lord, although more than once Carter caught a glimpse of what might have been the clawed, snouted shadow from his odyssey with Slaader. There was definitely an appalling, cosmic loneness that left Carter feeling bound and gagged as discordant echoes of human voices yelling for his blood tore through him like a descending pendulum. Almost all was an alien and perturbing kaleidoscope of familiar elements overlaid upon one another without regard for Time and Space's bedrocks with images of curious clarity mingling baffling heterogeneity occasionally bubbling up. Once Carter seemed prone in a pit surrounded by a rabble with straggling locks and cocked hats that glowered and spat upon him. Elsewhen Carter was inside an ostensibly old house, although details and inhabitants varied constantly while doors and windows shifted with the flux of mobile objects, rendering identifying rooms, furniture, or faces nearly hopeless, yet he sensed several of the inhabitants were members of the Harris family through the centuries. The faces returned with him to the cellar, where, instead of Norton, there was Elliott gawking at Carter with mounting horror. Another face also joined the swarm, pale as a skull with hungry teeth and glittering eyes set in dark sockets. At first it kept to the shadows but then drew nearer, its proximity in tune with a smothering sensation that pervaded like a presence possessing his vital processes. Overpowered by the onslaught of so many people Carter felt himself surrendering to a feeling like a bug in a fly trap ... being absorbed ... unable to physically hold his center as Elliott screams and flees and abandons him until Norton caught Carter's arm.

"Cut it out."

Carter gulped, filling his lungs. He felt confused and fatigued. "What?"

"Sitting there like you're sleeping ... scowly faced ... mumbling French ... not appreciated." Norton sounded roused, as if he had also been dozing.

"What did I say?"

"'*Souffle.*' '*Étouffer.*' Some words like that. High school French was long ago." Norton's head drooped and his breathing soon fell into the shallow and regular rhythm of incipient sleep.

You're by yourself again, but that was not accurate. Norton was still there, if only in body. So were several Roulets beneath the hard earth floor, one possibly restless.

"The apocrypha claims that corpses resting here never decay, but lay firm and fat, as if sleeping, as they wait for the stars to be right again."

Warren had dipped so deeply into forbidden things that Carter wondered if it ever dawned on the tyrant-monster that one such corpse might lie nearer to his serfdom than Big Cypress Swamp. A corpse that might have grown who-knew-how-big after centuries of life-sucking. Warren had said that the apocrypha vanished after being brought to New England from France, but did not say when this was or who had brought it and why. Could the dread apocrypha have belonged to Etienne Roulet? If so, did it vanish after the mob buried Paul and his family? In the end, none of that mattered to Warren.

"Harley, what's going on?"

"Nothing we can't handle."

Wrong.

Perhaps Warren should have heeded the Book of Isaiah:

Then man's arrogance should be humbled
And the pride of men brought low.
... And men shall enter caverns in the rock
And holes in the ground ...

Or perhaps Friedrich von Juntz's warning near the end of *Unaussprechlichen Kulten* against disturbing sleeping things that seem dead, but only lay waiting for some blind fool to wake them. Only Warren knows what—if anything—happened to him beneath the necropolis, but Carter did not escape that anonymous city of the dead unscathed.

"You have a visitor."

"The police again?

"Harley Warren. He was worried."

Not that worried, it turned out, and Carter being committed would have pushed the young man into Abaddon if Slaader had not been there to catch him.

"Not many know what wonders are open to them in the stories and visions of their youth."

During Carter's odyssey he returned to Elm Mountain the summer after his father died. For five years prior to that Carter's father had been a patient at Mass Hospital. The story went that Carter's father had succumbed to a permanent paralytic state brought on by overwork and insomnia, but people closest to Carter and his mother, such as the Pickmans, knew better. Mother and son had moved in with his father's affluent parents in Providence at their insistence, but, when the school year ended and Carter's mother was still incapacitated by grief and shame, his great-uncle Christopher and great-aunt Martha invited the boy to spend his vacation with them. Carter's paternal grandfather—who was becoming like a father to him—wrote often. In one letter he mentioned that his brother kept several heirlooms—some dating back to Carter's Elizabethan namesake and his heir Edmund—stored in the farmhouse's attic that the boy would find interesting.

"There is much to learn for those who care or dare to look."

Slaader escorted Carter to many different places and phases during their odyssey, which lasted lifetimes, but—like Scrooge's journeys with the Three Spirits—Slaader accomplished it in one night. One of those was the place beyond Space inhabited by the sentient gases. These beings, Carter learned, are conceived with genetic memories near the event horizon of black hole nebulae traversing our infinities, where they are swaddled in meteoroids like sand grains in pearls. On rare occasions a meteoroid is expelled rather than drawn through the singularity, and some of these wayward incubators wind up on populated worlds, much to the detriment of some of its inhabitants. If released the gases will sustain themselves on the most convenient form, matter, or energy available until they are strong enough to find a way back to their own space.

"Joe Slaader is dead."

When Carter heard this on his last night at Mass Hospital, the young man was stupefied and did not want to believe it as Slaader explained.

"His gross body could not adjust between ethereal life and planet life nor bear the active intellect of cosmic entity, making him my diurnal prison. Joe Slaader was more animal than man, but in truth we are both exiles and I empathized with his pangs to return to the life he knew in the wilderness he loved. 'Captivity to a sailor accustomed to the boundless ocean is a worse punishment than human punishment ever merited.' He knew this as well as I and is better dead, but his withering and deficiencies made it possible for you and I to find each other, a priceless gift for which I am most grateful."

"You saved me from myself." It was the most proper way Carter could think to say thank you.

"And you have been my only friend on this planet. I am your brother in light and friend in the cosmos, but there is nothing left here but a corpse. I am at last free to go as a Nemesis bearing just and blazingly cataclysmic vengeance."

This was new. At no time had Slaader previously evidenced any sort of animosity against anyone or anything.

"I will not speak of my oppressor. Again I caution how little the earth self ought to know life and its extent for its tranquility, and the cosmic and planet souls should rightly never meet. Because you and I have floated together in the effulgent valley, I shall confess that I have striven for eons to meet and conquer a tyrant, only to be held back by bodily encumbrances. Trevor. Athib. Kuranes. And many more. My own legion whose line ends with Slaader even as the end draws nigh for the thing that laughs and mocks. You on earth have felt my oppressor's ominous presence and named it Algol."

Dizziness assailed Carter, as if he had abruptly wafted into immeasurable depths and lost orientation.

"We shall meet again once we complete our quests. Watch for me in the sky near the Demon-Star and watch for a Guide for you. A terrible Guide. The Guardian of the Gate who waits for the Man of Truth who possessed a key to the ivory gates only to lose it. Recall the key and return it to the Inner Gate you found as a boy."

Carter's ears tickled as Slaader's syllabification weakened or faded.

"You have seen that there are twists of Time and Space, of vision and reality, which only a dreamer can divine. Remember that when you watch for me."

Randolph Carter sits alone with his thoughts.

Thoughts that fixate on what might lie below them as his companion's breathing softens and the pale-lit cellar grows quiet as a grave. The febrile odor persists, but not a murmur is audible except the confused running of his own blood, hardly loud enough to mask his tinnitus. His skin begins to sweat. Worry and fear whirl helter-skelter, shearing his nerves as his mind and superstition clash, the archetypal conflict and one in which—as Norton pointed out earlier—superstition usually and quite easily holds its own.

A sound breaks the silence.

Not a human sound.

A creaking like tightening rope, most probably issuing from the sinuous roots but possibly from the redolent patch. Or perhaps it was a droning like the tingling of glass coming from the fungi that shined like ground mist in the waning hours of the night.

Carter's tinnitus loudens the way it will before his ears pop on an airplane as Norton twitches in his chair. Sensing something is coming, Carter begins recording using his smart phone as perspiration breaks out on the sleeper's forehead and Norton mumbles words and phrases in guttural French from *Al Azif*, including "Nyarlathotep" and a couplet Alhazred composed after dreaming of The Nameless City:

"Ce n'est pas mort quit peut coucher eternal.
Et avec des aéons estranges, même la mort peut mourir."

Norton's breathing becomes stertorous and his twitching intensifies. A feral caul covers his face and his lids flutter, revealing eyes unlike his own but of many different men as Carter cautiously switches on the anode ray tube again.

* * *

6

"Randolph Carter dares to look beyond the Veil?"

Creaking roots and tingling fungi seem to speak through Norton, melding into a voice calling as if from some deep grotto, impressing Carter's ears the way gelatinous or glutinous matters impress the fingers. The words—so similar to Slaader's invitation—upset him as Carter glimpses something out of the corner of his eye. He turns to watch a subtle, trembling, and dimly luminous haze steam up from the manlike patch, over which it develops suggestions of form, half-human, half-monstrous, with a rugose insectoid head.

"Are you the shadow I spied in my dreams?" Carters asks.

"I am not!" comes the reply. "Shadows in dreams reveal more about the dreamer than those dreamt of."

Carter decides he will try to decipher that later. "Are you Paul Roulet?"

"Call him my host."

"Who, and what are you?" Carter demands.

"A terrible Guide, perhaps?" 'Norton' laughs as the yellow and diseased corpse-light bubbles and laps to a gigantic height, seemingly all eyes, wolfish and mocking. "Surely I'm no less than that keen visage amongst the insubstantial countenances you saw in your dream. I spotted you, too. You have no secrets from me."

You're no less like talking to Warren.

The phantasm may have sensed Carter's doubts for it immediately tells him: "I am from the past. I am visitant to the faithful sons of the first men who worship those that fell to this world before its foundations were laid and its seas shut up. I am counselor to some that seek our secrets and headsman to any who fail to guard them. And who, and what are you? Orange or lemon? Candle or chopper? Or Man of Truth, wishing to return to the small lands of lost dreams? Are you one who seeks greater freedom to arise to other desires and curiosities, or do you ache to be something more?"

As 'Norton' speaks a thin stream of mist twines from the phantasm's head to envelope him. The man's twitching erupts into convulsions as his skin blackens and slithers with faces that Carter—repulsed and horrified—recognizes from the Harris line: masculine and feminine, adult and infantile, and other features old and young, coarse and refined, familiar and unfamiliar. Carter also recognizes one face belonging to Whipple.

In that moment Carter discovers the monstrous not only can paralyze but affront.

"Leave him be!"

"What refuge or resource does such a one deserve? You were warned of a terrible Guide."

For an unforgivable instant Carter considers the circumstances and then remembers: *"Eddie Upton died."*

The instant passes, as does the time for questions

Randolph Carter stuffs his phone in a coat pocket, snatches the paper sack, and grabs three salutes as he kneels between Norton and the vampiric vapor. Turning on the toaster, Carter touches the fuses against the glowing nichrome elements and drops the sputtering M-80s into the sack before flinging it away. It passes through the phantasm and lands on top of the patch as he slams the anode ray housing into the carrying case, grabs its handle, and reaches for Norton.

Carter feels the report through his skin before he hears it.

Dirt, pebbles, and bits of toadstools and Indian pipes pelt away like hornets with stingers the size of knitting needles.

Hurling open the door to drag Norton outside, Carter glances back, but all he sees through the smoke and dust is a man-size crater in front of the fireplace.

7

Henry Pratt is puzzled.

"This can't be right."

Lon Creighton, the excavation foreman, takes another sip of long black. "Find something?"

"Yes, but ..." Pratt stops pushing the ground penetrating radar, a device resembling a lawn mower with a DVD player mounted on its handlebar, next to the fresh hole near the fireplace.

Justin Beahm, an archaeologist with Massachusetts's Department of Historic Preservation, looks at the GRP's high resolution touch screen. "You don't sound very sure of yourself."

"It's more like I'm not sure what I've found."

Creighton looks, too. Not being trained on this equipment, what he sees "Looks like a blob. What do you think it is?"

"It could be a mass grave, I suppose."

Beahm: "That's my thinking. The attenuation is certainly right for it."

Creighton: "That's good? Right? Isn't that what we're looking for?"

"We're looking for bodies, Lon."

"So ...?"

Pratt pushes buttons on the touch screen to bring up different images. "Look for yourself. It doesn't matter if I use depth slices or line views with small/shallow, medium size/depth, or large/deep targets enhancements. I've been adjusting the dielectric permittivity and electrical conductivity as well as taken into account for reflection, scattering, spreading losses, and system performance. Whatever I do, it all comes back the same."

"That you've found a bunch of bodies buried together?"

"No. That there's one big body buried under this cavity."

Creighton nods. "How big are you talking?"

"About three times your size."

"Really? I'm bigger than your average bear."

"Yes, you are, Yogi."

Creighton takes another sip. "I bet it's a statue. The oversize kind you see in cemeteries. Maybe whoever was playing around in here last night buried it as a joke."

"Well, setting aside every other argument against that running through my noggin for the moment, stone such as granite has a velocity of 0.13, whereas the velocity of these radar signals are lower and closer to what you'd expect to get from human remains."

"It was just a suggestion." Another nod followed by another sip. "Well, the City's not paying us to guess. Let me grab a couple of boys off the street and let's see what you've found."

As Creighton leaves the cellar, Pratt comments on proceeding with any exhumation before taking more time to get permission from any next of kin. "Even with a court order, this could come back to bite us."

"Not us. The City. They're the ones footing the $2000 per body bill."

"We'd be dragged into it somehow."

"To present testimony, maybe, but it's no big deal. I had to do it once when I was working in another state. A farmer plowed some bones up from an Indian burial site no one knew was on his property. No one was to blame, but you couldn't tell that to the American Indian Movement, and back then that was not a group you wanted to irritate. AIM was fit to be tied until I and several others in the Historical Preservation Office testified that the state was obeying the Native American Graves Protection and Repatriation Act to make sure all the remains buried on that farmer's land would be presented to a culturally affiliated tribe. Of course, we didn't tell anyone we were storing those bones in a cardboard box next to my desk until which tribe that was could be established."

"I can't say that makes me feel better."

"Then take solace in the fact that the City Attorney is right. There's enough exigent evidence to proceed under the presumption that any search for next of kin would prove a waste of time. First, Carrington Harris has assured us that his ancestors never buried anyone on this land. Second, scholars have been investigating the Jacques Roulet case for nearly four centuries, more than a few of whom have documented being unable to locate any living Roulet descendants in France or America."

Creighton returns with two crewmen, Wayne Amsler and Ed Sherman. Unable to employ even a mini-excavator or rubber tired backhoe in the confined space, the three bring shovels and mattocks as well as a pair of dual LED worklights on tripods. After extending the hole about one foot down, Sherman complains about the odor and Beahm informs him, "According to our historical architect, it's always been a part of the house. Especially down here."

Pratt remarks, "It's probably all these toadstools."

"A lot of people think that, but the smell remains even when no fungi are growing."

Amsler coughs to stifle a gag. "Maybe something's seeping from them into soil. Whatever it is, the smell's getting worse the deeper we go."

"Wayne's right," Creighton says. "I think we ought to play this smart." The foreman orders hazardous materials suits brought in for himself, Amsler, and Sherman, and self-contained breathing apparatus for Pratt and Beahm. Creighton also orders work on Benefit Street halted until whatever is under the cellar is uncovered.

During the next three hours the diggers swelter inside their hazmat suits as the twin worklights not only obscure any luminescence still emanating from the mushrooms but a burgeoning sunbeam seeping closer to the pit as the morning drags on. Just as Creighton is getting ready to order hydraulic vertical shores be brought in so they can start bracing, Amsler stops digging. "I don't like this, boss."

Creighton and Sherman turn his way as the foreman asks, "What don't you like?"

"Where I'm standing."

"What about where you're standing?"

"It's real soft, boss."

"Get out and let me look. You, too, Ed."

Amsler and Sherman clamber out as Creighton begins scraping dirt from Amsler's spot, the side nearest the fireplace. Before long: "There's something here."

"What is it?"

"I don't know. I mean, I see it, but I can't say that's helping." Creighton's scraping reveals a roughly cylindrical blue-white object tapering from a broadest diameter of two feet. "It feels like petrolatum." The semi-putrid surface of the object is fishy and glassy with hints of transparency. "Might be an old stove pipe that's turned soft. There's a bend in the middle of it." Creighton stops. "I don't like this, either. Ed, call Chris in the M.E.'s office." This is Christopher Jones, the medical examiner's liaison in regards to the Harris House excavation. "Tell him we're not digging any more until someone comes down here and tells me what we've landed." Creighton begins climbing out of the pit when the dirt floor trembles and he slips back in.

Pratt, staring at the touch screen, mewls, "No way."

Beahm: "What?"

"The big body shifted."

Sherman reaches to help Creighton. "We must have jarred something loose."

Amsler does the same. "Grab our hands, boss."

Creighton starts to but tumbles as the cellar floor trembles again in accordance with the blob on the touch screen shifting once more. Six feet from the side of the pit furthest from the fireplace the earth ripples, mushrooms rolling over the ground like flotsam in a wave. Inside the pit the blue-white thing slithers as the dirt beneath Creighton quivers. "Something's happening down here!" Before the foreman can move, a light slaps Creighton. Without thinking, he lifts a hand to shade his eyes.

Unnoticed in the confusion and worklights, the sunbeam has reached the pit where it blinds Creighton and douches the blue-white thing. A titanic roar echoes beneath the cellar, the floor quakes, and the blue-white thing bursts, spewing rancid jelly on Creighton.

An instant later the ground settles and the cellar is silent.

Pratt: "It's gone!"

Beahm checks the touch screen. "Henry's right. Our big body's not registering."

Unnoticed by the dumbfounded men, the shimmer from the toadstools and pipes fades as the fungi shrivel. As Creighton's crewmen on the street rush into the cellar, the pale grass and strange weeds on the Harris House lawn likewise wither. Over the next few days birds begin to nest in the gnarled boughs of the misshapen trees, which, for the first summer in memory, bear small, sweet apples. Meanwhile in Arkham, light returns to the gray EB patients as each one takes an inexplicable turn for the better. After all of man's medical devices have failed, the sickness simply but indefatigably ends with no more explanation than how it started.

* * *

8

"Randolph Carter isn't here."

Patrolman Morris is reporting over his handheld transceiver. Accompanying him is Patrolman Leigh Hunt, who is riding with Morris until Lewis is cleared to return to field work.

"No chance he's inside the old Carter place?" McClure asks.

"We checked it. Somebody definitely entered the house recently, but no one's there now. There are also no signs of forced entry, so my money's on it being Carter and he had a key."

"And the Valley Cab driver positively identified Carter and the location he dropped him off?"

"Ten-four to both. Old Miskatonic Road doesn't come any closer to the house then the spot he showed us."

"What's your 20 now?"

"Outside the Snake Den. Thanks to that rain last night we could follow tracks from the farmhouse up here that led inside. Haven't found any leading out, though, and, as far as me and my new sidekick can tell, the cave's empty."

"I'll have a K-9 unit join you and see what they can find. You're a good policeman, Al, but you're no Natty Bumppo."

"Copy that."

Two hours earlier, Pickman contacts the Arkham Police, claiming to be concerned about Carter because of a recent anxiety attack and an even more recent release from the Massachusetts Hospital School. A few hours before this, Pickman is perplexed to find a moving container in front of Carter's house and even more surprised that Derby is inside organizing the packing and removal of their friend's belongings. "Playing cuckoo while Carter's away?"

Derby continues working. "What are you doing here?"

"I was stretching my legs and thought someone was looting Carter. Looks like I was right."

"Nothing more or less is going than what it looks like."

"What happened to you brooding over your lady fair?" Derby had spent most of the previous afternoon at The White Ship worrying about how he had not heard from Asenath since the quarantine's cancellation.

"Elton set me straight on that."

"Basil gave you advice?" Unlike the classic cliché bartender, Elton rarely proffered anyone advice.

"Not me directly, but I heard him."

"Okay, whatever that means." Pickman looks around again. "So what does go on here?"

"Dolph requested I put his things in storage for him."

Now it was Pickman's turn to feel concerned. "When did he do that? He's all right?"

"He's fine, as far as I know."

"So why all this? Is the hospital keeping him until his lease runs out?"

Derby blinks before asking, "Hasn't he contacted you?"

"We haven't talked since I told him about Eddie."

"Terrific." Derby scowls. "That probably means he hasn't told Daniel and Dinah either."

"Told them what?"

"He was released last week."

Pickman staggers. In a raspy voice: "When did you find that out?"

"He called me the day before he got out. He needed a place to stay until the quarantine was lifted, and I knew how to contact a mutual friend in Providence."

"Who's that?"

"Aldin Norton."

"His old J-School roommate? Carter hasn't mentioned him in years."

"Apparently he didn't want to stay with family and he couldn't think of anyone else."

Pickman wags his head. "He doesn't have many relatives, but, yeah, that makes sense."

"They don't get along?"

"They're different types."

"Are they all lawyers like his cousin Ernest?"

"You mean Aspinwall? How do you know about him?"

"Dolph asked me to FedEx his cousin his instructions on what to do with his estate after I finish here."

"Where is he going?"

"I don't know. All he said was that he was leaving Arkham."

Pickman counts to five, and then, "This doesn't make any sense! He has one more year and a dissertation to complete for his doctorate! What did he tell the school?"

"I don't know, R.U."

"All the years we've known each other! Why would he leave without discussing it with me?"

"Again, I don't know."

"Well, is there anything you do know?"

Derby picks a wooden box off the corner desk and holds it out. "I know he wants you to have this."

"What is it?"

"Let me repeat: I don't know." Derby makes a prudish face. "It smells like a Moroccan souk."

Pickman accepts the box only to jerk back his hand as if shocked.

"Splinter?"

Remembering Derby's interest in the *Necronomicon* and recognizing many of the grimoire's most grotesque carvings, Pickman lies: "It looks like sandalwood. I'm allergic to sandalwood oil."

Derby knows better but plays along. "I suppose that would explain its fragrance, but the box is dried out. Probably kilned. Anyway, it's too yellow for sandalwood. If it's not oak, I'm almost positive it's Lebanon cedar."

"You're an arborist now?" Pickman removes the silk scarf around his neck to grab the box as much as cover its scrollwork, but the bottom of the box drops open in the exchange. An envelope with *Pickman* typed on it and a discolored parchment drift out. Pickman snatches the parchment and he and Derby peruse it. "Feels old."

"Exquisite chirography. Can you read it?"

"Like I told Gilman, I'm no paleographer." Pickman is positive, however, that, while no priest in Thebes could read the parchment, there are some parts of it he can, including mention of the messenger Nyarlathotep.

Derby picks up the envelope and hands it to Pickman. "Maybe you'll have better luck with this."

"Maybe I will." Pickman turns to leave. "And maybe you can let me know how things go with Aspinwall." Outside, he turns the corner and walks down Parsonage Street before he opens the envelope. Inside is a smaller blue envelope addressed to *The Uptons* and the folded sketch he drew of Carter at Mass Hospital. Unfolding the sketch, he finds a letter from Carter on the back.

"MY DEAR PICKMAN," it says, "I apologize for not presenting my farewell in person. Recent events—along with an heirloom that has been wrapped in the accompanying parchment and kept in this box—have set me on an inexorable journey. I fear my hole-and-corner release from the Hospital School and my departure from Arkham will give pain to my friends, especially you, so I leave the box and parchment with you in the trust that you know—or are at least beginning to suspect—that there is a trace of certain ancient things linked with all the laws of Time and Space. My journey will have very dark descents—something you may know about, judging by your paintings—but I aim to uncover this continuity's mysteries. I have been warned, however, that there are those who guard such secrets and this makes remaining in Arkham impossible. I am therefore entrusting the storage of my property to Derby and its disposition to my cousin in Chicago. I ask you to deliver the blue envelope to Daniel and Dinah. I wish I could have been with them when Eddie passed but I am confident he is in a good place. Also please give my greetings to the other good fellows of The Shipwright Circle and to Basil, and believe me to be, my dear fellow,
"Very sincerely yours,
"Randolph Carter."

Struck numb, Pickman reads the letter twice more before returning it to its envelope and slipping the envelope into a pocket of his business-man spring jacket. A kindle of indignation almost erupts but Pickman stamps it down and concentrates on delivering Carter's missive.

Instead of walking west to the Uptons's reconditioned red brick Federal on the corner of Boundary and Saltonstall Streets, Pickman makes his way east to French Hill Street and then south straight into Christchurch Cemetery, passing under the gilded words from the Book of Revelations writ across the arched entranceway:

"Blessed Are the Dead Who Die in the Lord"

Sounds like cold comfort to me, he thinks.

Following a rutted carriage road towards a capacious willow, the cemetery seems peaceful, but the further Pickman travels the more he feels like he did tramping through Cold Island. It does not help that graveyards always play havoc with his afflatus, even more so after dark when his mind's eye cascades with mephitic monsters dancing amongst tombstones and his fancy conjures images of tumefying graves expanding through the inner earth, metamorphing into passages betwixt the surface and primordial nether regions

Score one for you, Carter. I do know something about dark descents.

Reaching the willow, Pickman pauses beside a clutter of weather-worn slate markers leaning near a drapery of narrow leaves. He keeks at the tombstone for a Thomas Bewick and its epigraph

Good Times
&
Bad Times
&
'all Times
Come Over

before drawing back the curtain and peering into the shady idyll beneath the tree's umbrella.

The air is as cool and pungent as an ancient Egyptian embalmer's shop. Daylight sifting through the catkins paints patterns of interlacing lines as if shining through a tracery. Eddie Upton lies here with every Upton who died before him since the seventeenth century, and—just as they have each afternoon since the health authorities finally permitted them to bury their boy—Dinah and Daniel sit together on a mossy stone bench, silent except for sometimes crying.

Pickman rubs his fingers over his jacket pocket as he closes the curtain.

Actually, Carter, I don't know anything.

Trooping to Boundary and Saltonstall, Pickman leaves the blue envelope in the Uptons's mailbox along with a note to contact him if they have any questions or just need to talk. Mission accomplished, irritation threatens to erupt again, and that is when Pickman calls the Arkham Police, prodding them into trying to find out where Carter has gone and if his friend is all right.

Shortly before dusk the previous evening at The White Ship, Derby is sulking at the Russell table while a crowd of students collected around the bar commiserate the cessation of the quarantine. One of them, Arthur Bellinger, a history major, puts minimum effort into lifting his weizen glass of blueberry wheat and intones: "To ontological anxiety."

Three people down from Bellinger, Conan Trelawney, a philosophy major attending Harvard Law School in the fall, slowly rolls his stange between his palms without a care that he is bringing his German Kölsch to room temperature. "Ontic anxiety is bad enough, but having now seen the 'vistas' that 'mock man's littleness'? It seems as if Heidegger's new autochthony is coming to pass, only through the microbe instead of technology."

Near the end of the bar, Hilda Oberstein, a non-traditional double major in computer science and art struggling to launch her own Internet fashion line, stares at her taster glass as she ponders indulging in another sample of Sam Adams Utopia. "I feel the same way. There's anxiety from fate and death on one hand and the anxiety from emptiness and meaningless on the other. All we're missing is anxiety from guilt and condemnation."

Trelawney: "You're forgetting survivor's guilt."

Oberstein slides slitted eyes his direction. "Thank you. Now my life's complete."

Elton inquires if anyone in the crowd needs a drink freshened.

Oberstein decides to splurge. "You only live once."

"Unless you're James Bond." Elton winks as he opens the kettle shaped bottle of 28 proof beer.

"I don't get you," Oberstein says.

"Double-oh-seven." Pours two fingers.

"I know who he is."

"*You Only Live Twice.*"

"That's one of his stories, right?"

"Before our time, I'm afraid" Trelawney chimes in.

Elton: "I'm afraid that cop-out ain't proprietary to your generation." His glare cows any comebacks. "It's also a poor man's haiku: 'Ya only live twice. Once when you're born. And once when ya stare death in the face.'"

Oberstein takes a sip and enjoys an alcohol burn illegal in fifteen states. "I guess we did do that."

Elton puts away the bottle. "I'm sorry, did ya come down with EB?"

"No."

"Then what death did ya face?"

Trelawney cuts in: "We were quarantined. Any of us—even you—could have contracted it. And let's not forget Halsey. Any of us could have ended up as one of his victims if we'd been at the wrong place at the wrong time."

"I see Basil's point," Bellinger says. "We were at risk, but that isn't the same thing as facing the immediate threat of death. Dodging a bullet in no way compares with being hit by it. We were never in genuine peril."

"It sure as hell counts in my book!" Oberstein insists. "Look, I can't help feeling grateful to whatever fate saved me from contracting EB or crossing Halsey's path, but I can't help feeling there isn't any point to anything in life when my life can come to an end just like that (snaps her fingers)."

Trelawney: "Impermanence is an absolute for everyone and everything in the universe."

"And whatever we do—no matter how well we do it—is always going to be rendered imperfect because the fact of non-being skulks in the background, waiting, forever and always, and we're powerless against it."

"My point precisely. Cases for the immortality of the soul have no argumentative power, but, even if they did, they'd still have no existential conviction. Even the most unsophisticated person is existentially aware of the loss of self that biological extinction implies. In the end, there is no purpose."

The students turn to Elton, who, listening with crossed arms, grumbles, "Are ya being serious or just bandying two dollar words?" Before the students can respond, "Look, I'm not a sophisticated person, but it seems to me the fact something isn't going to be around forever makes it precious. Besides, who the hell knows what you're doing now, except maybe the folks who matter most in yer lives? How would living an eternity change that? Thank God for self-preservation. None of us would be here without it. But don't mix it up with what's worthwhile. Again, that could just be my upbringing talking. I'm a sod who's satisfied with his lot in life, but I haven't always been. People change and some grow more accepting of the way things are. Right now, though I've got bills to pay and people that depend on me, so I'll let you all get back to it." And Elton gets back to work.

Outside The White Ship, West is sitting on the boat slip, which is furnished for *al fresco* dining. A chilly breeze blowing off the Miskatonic is discouraging the other customers, so West has his pick of tables. Deep in thought, not really drinking his wine cooler, West watches the waterway without really paying attention.

"Dr. West."

West opts not to respond.

"We need to talk."

Still no response.

"My name is Robert Suydam. I represent several colleagues of your former neighbor, the late Dr. Hector Muñoz."

Not wanting to encourage, West maintains his stony silence.

"This need only take a moment." Suydam sits.

West looks but does not recognize the lupine-looking man blessed with a physique of coiled energy and a splendid Phoenician purple suit, an ebony cane with silver handle casually clutched in one hand. Nevertheless, "I know why you're here."

"Excellent."

"And you're wasting your time. I don't have what you're looking for."

Suydam grins. "Dr. Muñoz had one friend during his last days. You. He saved your life when you were nothing but a stranger to him. How is your heart, by the way?"

West turns his face back towards the Miskatonic. "Better than ever, thanks to him."

"All he prescribed in return was that you transmit some documents to those I represent."

"Which doesn't change the fact that I cannot provide something I do not possess."

Suydam's grin grows as hard as a car's grill. "If you insist."

"I insist because it's true."

"Let us hope not. If it is, I am almost certain those who Dr. Muñoz's documents were intended for will insist that I speak with the police about Allan Halsey."

West almost looks insouciant. "The Dean?"

"It is public record you and a friend assisted a rather robust stranger into your apartment not long after Halsey had his car accident and vanished. If not for the recent outbreak I'm sure the police would have paid more attention to that or that the residence where Halsey had his initial nosh and was subsequently captured is conveniently located near the site of both that accident and your apartment. Now that Arkham is returning to normal, it shouldn't take more than a nudge to get them investigating those coincidences. After all, who isn't curious to find out why one of the east coast's most respected practitioners abruptly devolved into a lurking beast?" Suydam stands. "Upon my oath, there's no desire on our part to encumber your experiments, Dr. West. Fanatics have their uses, and in more ways than one your efforts are continuing our late colleague's animus against death. If anything we encourage such efforts, though from afar." Inhales. Exhales. "A very pleasant evening. Brisk. Dr. Muñoz would have appreciated it." Walks away. "I'll be in touch."

A few days earlier, Norton's vibrating phone rouses him.

He is discombobulated after dreaming about being buried in a big hole by an angry mob of early New Englanders and then floating like Marley's Ghost through a house whose walls and doors did not have the decency to stay in one place before winding up in the Harris House cellar with a cloud of faces, including a disturbing one that looked like something out of a Japanese horror film.

Waking begrudgingly, Norton expects to find himself in the cellar, but he is lying in his bed in Pearl Street still dressed in the clothes he wore to Harris House. Digging his phone out of his pocket, Norton recognizes Carter's number and answers. "How did I get home?"

"I helped you. How are you feeling?"

Norton is sore all over. When he looks his body is freckled with bruises and blotched with dirt. "Like I do the day after every Mardi Gras. I don't recall drinking anything or getting in a dirt clod fight. What happened?"

"Don't you remember anything?"

Norton tries, but, "Last thing I recall is you talking in your sleep. In French. Very annoying."

"So you intimated. You nodded off yourself after that."

Makes himself sit up. "Those smelly fumes must have got the better of me."

"Don't feel bad. They almost got the better of me."

"So where are you?"

"On Benefit Street. I wanted to see how things were going with the excavation."

"Good thinking. I ought to get down there, too."

"No rush. It looked like they ran into a snag, but now it seems as if they're back on track."

"What sort of snag was it?"

"I can't say. It was in the cellar and the public isn't being allowed near enough to see in there. Maybe you can ask your confidential source."

"I will. Are you heading back now? I want details on what happened after I zonked out. I don't suppose you recorded anything?"

"As a matter of fact I did, but there's someplace I need to go next."

"All right. You can show me later. I'm going to grab a shower and try to rinse the cobwebs out of my brain."

"Good idea. And thanks again for opening your home to me."

"What are friends for?"

"Maybe, but I'm not sure I would have done the same if someone called out of the blue the way I did. I truly will miss that view." Disconnects.

Norton lurches halfway to his bathroom before Carter's last words get him wondering. Weaving into the living room, he finds the anode ray case beside the sofa with Carter's fedora on top of it. Carter's black suitcase is gone. A sawbuck is tucked into the fedora's hatband with a note: "Please return the case to Traux. You're probably right about Warren, so paying off our bet now. Do as you wish with my hat. Don't think I need it any longer."

* * *

9

The astronomer is confused.

Professor J. Kenneth Kuntz, director of the Ladd Observatory at Brown University, suspects Randolph Carter may also be confused.

"'Has there been any recent activity near Beta Persei?'" Kuntz repeats Carter's question.

"No, sir, near Algol."

"Beta Persei is the Bayer designation for Algol, son."

"Oh, I see." Carter makes a mental note to look up the definition of Bayer designation later. "Has there been any recent activity near Beta Persei then?"

"How recent?"

"This past week."

"Nothing except the regular dip in Algol's magnitude from 2.1 to 3.4 every 2 days, 20 hours, and 49 minutes."

"I see." Carter nods. "I have no idea what that means."

"Well, I'm afraid I have no idea what you mean by 'activity.'"

"To be honest, I'm not sure myself. A very good teacher of mine told me to watch for...something...near Algol."

"I see. That clears things up splendidly, but there's been no unusual activity near Algol for over a century."

"Did something happen then?"

"Oh, yes. It was in all the newspapers." The men are standing on a brick walkway leading to the front steps of a squat, thick-necked Victorian brick building with copper dome. Pruned and polished landscaping bracket the walkway while large apple trees blossom along a broad sidewalk circumferencing the observatory on Tin Top Hill at the corner of Hope and Doyle. Kuntz points towards the northwest center of the night sky. "On 21 February 1901, a Scottish clergyman and amateur astronomer named Thomas David Anderson was the first to discover Nova Persei 1901 right about there."

"Did you say 'nova'? Algol exploded?"

"No." Kuntz moves his finger. "It's that bright star in the Perseus constellation." Looks at Carter. "Beta Persei is a multiple star consisting of three stars orbiting one another, but Nova Persei 1901 was the brightest nova in modern history until Nova Aquilae 1918 came along. At first Nova Persei outshone Capella, but within a couple of weeks it had faded only to begin displaying fairly regular outbursts. For the last two score years these outbursts have occurred approximately every three years and they last around two months." Lowers his hand. "I'm afraid that's all I've got."

"I see. Well, thank you for speaking with me, sir."

"I'm sorry I couldn't be more help, but that's Beta Persei for you. Besides being one of the fifteen Behenian stars, Algol is considered to be one of the unluckiest stars in the sky."

Instead of being disheartened, Carter appeared to be encouraged. "I've heard something like that, too. I've also heard there are twists of Time and Space, so who knows? Thank you again, Professor."

In the days that follow the Arkham police are able to find out that Carter departed Providence on a bus to Lefferts Corner, New York the morning after speaking to Kuntz. There he purchased an urn at Chambers & Grubbs Mortuary that he donated to the relatives of Joe Slaader, an inmate at the Massachusetts Hospital School who died the night before Carter's release. Carter then took a bus to Arkham, where he made his arrangements with Derby. On May Eve Carter hired the Valley Cab to drive him around town and Christchurch Cemetery, where he visited Eddie Upton's grave, before dropping him off on Old Miskatonic Road. The K-9 Unit confirmed that Carter visited his family's farmhouse before walking to the Snake Den, at which point the dog lost Carter's trail.

10

At last the key was mine to those vague visions
Of secret spires and twilight woods that brood
Dim in the gulfs beyond this earth's precisions,
Lurking as memories of infinitude.

- III. The Key, *Fungi from Yuggoth*

GRIST

FOUNTS
Beyond the Wall of Sleep
Nyarlathotep
The Plague-Daemon
The Shunned House
The Silver Key
The Statement of Randolph Carter
Through the Gate of the Silver Key
The Unnamable

HONOURABLE MENTIONS
At the Mountains of Madness
Celephaïs
The Colour Out of Space
The Dreams in the Witch House
The Dunwich Horror
From the Dark
Fungi from Yuggoth
The Horror at Red Hook
In the Crypt
The Nameless City
The Shadow over Innsmouth
The Shadow Out of Time
The Thing on the Doorstep

A GOOD CAST IS WORTH REPEATING
(or, "My collection of W's is a fine one.")

THE SHIPWRIGHT CIRCLE

RANDOLPH CARTER: Graduate student, antiquarian, historian, and research assistant to Professor Harley Warren. Childhood friend of R. U. Pickman.

EDWARD PICKMAN DERBY: Occultist and poet. Unofficial little brother of Daniel Upton.

FRANK ELWOOD: Graduate student, mathematician and physicist.

WALTER GILMAN: Graduate student, mathematician, physicist, and folklorist.

RICHARD UPTON (R.U.) PICKMAN: Graduate student. Artist. Childhood friend of Randolph Carter.

DANIEL UPTON: Architect, architectural historian, and artist. Husband of Dinah Upton, father of Edward Derby Upton, unofficial older brother of Edward Derby.

DINAH UPTON: Associate Director of Miskatonic University's Admissions Office. Wife of Daniel Upton, mother of Edward Derby Upton.

MISKATONIC UNIVERSITY

HENRY ARMITAGE: Dean of Libraries.

ARTHUR BELLINGER: Undergraduate majoring in History.

PETER COLLINS: Resident, Medical School.

MATTHEW ELLIOTT: Undergraduate majoring in Architecture. Nephew of Elihu Whipple.

ALLAN HALSEY: Dean of Miskatonic University's Faculty of Medicine and Medical School.

CONAN TRELAWNEY: Pre-law undergraduate majoring in Philosophy.

HILDA OBERSTEIN: Undergraduate majoring in Computer Science and Art. Owner of an internet fashion line.

ASENATH WAITE: Undergraduate majoring in medieval metaphysics. Daughter of the late Ephraim Waite, noted occultist.

DR. WALDRON: Head of Student Health.

HARLEY WARREN: Doctor of Psychology and Parapsychology, profiler.

HERBERT WEST: Resident, Medical School.

ARKHAM, MASS.

TED ALLISON: Detective, Arkham Police Department.

MR. BANACZEK.: Witch House owner.

CHRISTOPHER CARTER (DECEASED): Randolph Carter's great-uncle.

GRANDFATHER CARTER (DECEASED): Randolph Carter's second father.

MARTHA CARTER (DECEASED): Randolph Carter's great-aunt.

BASIL ELTON: Proprietor of The White Ship Tavern. Maritime historian.

CHRIS GERBER: Security guard. Retired policeman.

LEIGH HUNT: Patrol officer, Arkham Police Department.

GEORGINA KALEM: Arkham resident.

ISABEL LEWIS: Patrol officer, Arkham Police Department.

KEN McCLURE: Dispatcher, Arkham Police Department.

ALFRED MORRIS: Patrol officer, Arkham Police Department.

JAMES REINERTSON: Upton family's pediatrician.

EDWARD DERBY UPTON: Son of Daniel and Dinah Upton.

MASSACHUSETTS HOSPITAL SCHOOL

HAROLD BARNARD: Abnormal psychiatrist.

LAWRENCE OLMSTEAD: Patient.

JOE SLAADER: Catskill hunter, trapper, current avatar for entity that becomes Randolph Carter's dreamland mentor.

PROVIDENCE, R.I.

WAYNE AMSLER: Crewman, Providence Street Department.

JUSTIN BEAHM: Archaeologist, Massachusetts Department of Historic Preservation.

LON CREIGHTON: Foreman for the Providence Street Department.

CARRINGTON HARRIS: Harris House owner.

J. KENNETH KUNTZ: Director of the Ladd Observatory at Brown University.

ALDIN NORTON: Journalist, *Providence Journal*. Undergraduate roommate of Randolph Carter.

HENRY PRATT: Crewman, Providence Street Department.

ED SHERMAN: Crewman, Providence Street Department.

ELIHU WHIPPLE: Uncle of Matthew J. Elliott. Physician and amateur historian.

OTHERS OF PARTCIULAR NOTE

HART CRANE: Lieutenant, Miami-Dade Police Department.

GARDNER, NAHUM (DECEASED): West Valley farmer.

SAM LOVEMAN: Lieutenant, Miami-Dade Police Department.

HECTOR MUÑOZ (DECEASED): Physician. Friend of Herbert West.

NYARLATHOTEP: Ageless emissary of the Outer Gods. Takes many forms.

ETIENNE ROULET (DECEASED): Descendant of Jacques Roulet of Caude.

PAUL ROULET (DECEASED): Son of Etienne Roulet.

ROBERT SUYDAM: Representative of associates of the late Dr. Hector Muñoz. Noted expert on medieval superstition.

HERBERT WEST - RESURRECTED

THE EMPTY HOUSE ON HARLEY STREET
(A Sequel to H. P. Lovecraft's *Grewsome Tales*)

AUTHOR'S NOTE: This short story is a sequel to the Lovecraft series better known currently as Herbert West - Reanimator *and is not associated with* Lovecraftian - SPJ

All of London is enthralled with Dr. Herbert.

Every day patients line up to be cured of their ails and specialists in all branches of medicine consult with him.

Prominent spiritualists confer with him as well while the grieving come to ask about lost loved ones.

A few folks have even claimed that Herbert resuscitated someone recently dead once or twice.

"Reanimating the dead? Preposterous!"

It does sound ludicrous, but rumors can be good for business so long as they do not take on a life of their own, so as Herbert's associate and spokesman I am always vigilant not to discourage the validity while pruning the voracity of such gossip.

Dr. Herbert may become a greater phenomenon than Franz Mesmer. Many people have indisputably benefited from seeing him, but I make sure nobody knows anything about him. It is critical—essential—that Herbert remain a blank canvas so people can make what they want of him. He never talks about himself or his past. His credentials are his knowledge and successes. Herbert has detractors and doubters, as great doctors and great conjure-men must, but so far no admonition or accusation can be heard over his accolades.

This grand old city has never seen anything like Dr. Herbert and odds are it never will again. I hope so, anyway, for reasons that may be good or awful.

* * *

I first made Herbert's acquaintance in a nightmare.

I had not been in London long, arriving late one winter after nearly being devoured by a rumor about me. I escaped America with my skin but not my reputation and needing to hide in a new country living a new kind of life

My new name is Levi Hip. My real name will remain my secret. I am revealing more than I care to already, beginning with that nightmare, which gave me no peace as it tugged at me like a divining rod. I have reason to suspect a few Londoners maybe suffered the same nightmare on the same night, but Fate or coincidence got me to Swain's Lane first where I was drawn to the Circle of Lebanon in Highgate Cemetery.

The only light at that late hour and that deep into the West Cemetery came from a waning crescent moon, but an ancient cedar obstructed its faint glimmer as I descended into that ring of tombs. This was not my first night-call on a graveyard so I brought along my flashlight, but I felt like a virgin pilgrim as I passed a procession of thresholds in the Egyptian style on the inner side and Classical on the outer until the course was blocked by a mostly prone trilithon with an iron hatch jutting out of the ground. My mind painted the rusty whirls on the hatch's surface into imps and spawns skittering across cuneiforms of threatful knowledge, but I continued apace as the hatch warped like a hot cooking sheet doused in cold water and dropped open to expose steps hewn from the bedrock banking far into the earth. I followed them down, unwilling to turn back. That's my excuse, anyway.

How many steps? Who knows? I lost count by the time I reached a rock-tomb with a wondrous curving ashlar wall of black khalkedon with white veins. The precision of the dress and the polish to the bricks was inhuman, and scrolled into this marvel by some Moving Finger was a name:

HERBERT WEST

My mind might have buckled under the absurdities of the moment if I hadn't been too busy fixating on the name, as anyone familiar with New England medicine would have. West was a graduate of the prestigious Miskatonic University Medical School, a colleague of the late Sir Eric Moreland Clapham-Lee (D.S.O.) and a volunteer officer with the Canadian Army Medical Corps during the Great War. During his relatively short career in Boston West had compiled a list of almost miraculous surgical successes along with a reputation for being obsessed with finding an excitant solution to revivify the dead, but about the time I abandoned the States I read West had apparently been murdered by his long-time associate.

I stared at that name on that wall. "This doesn't make sense."

What made even less sense was my growing compulsion to get at the other side of that wall. Something there needed to be released, but even if I had the proper tools the wall struck me as impregnable. I could feel no chink or weak spot as I ran my hands over the silky bricks, which were unexpectedly warm and almost moist, but as if guided by a hunch I pressed my palms against the brick with the "H," stepped back, and it slid back with me, easy and light as a drawer, releasing an effluence of queer light. I slid out more bricks, not able or wanting to stop despite seeing something like this in my nightmare. Some sort of ancient masonry had been deconstructed from behind as the same queer kind of light gushed out along with a shambling legion of the damned. Was my dream turning into a premonition? I didn't believe in such things, but was anything happening believable? Only illumination escaped through my aperture, however, and as soon as I could slip through I did.

The candlepower was too much for me to make out any details of the other side.

All I could see for certain was Dr. Herbert West.

To say he was worse for wear is an understatement and to say I was amazed he was alive much less conscious even more so. Instead of being afraid, though, I was fascinated, and I like to think we hit it off from the start.

"I need your help," Herbert said after I introduced myself. "There's somewhere I must be. Now."

An indefatigable fire kindled in his blue eyes. I admired that, given the circumstances.

"Well, I've come this far. In for a penny ..."

* * *

Less than four miles north of Swain's Lane is Harley Street, a hub of medical practioners, surgeons and hospitals, and a few doors down from the office of Edward Bach stands Agar House. No one had lived there since its owner died in the war, but Agar House was far from abandoned. Something watched over the place.

Herbert became my new divining rod after we left the cemetery, and he was adamant we enter the house unseen, so I found a narrow passage off an adjoining street that took us to a wooden gate that led into Agar House's deserted backyard. I would have picked the rear door's lock next, only it was open. "So much for sneaking in." I asked Herbert if he was still game for going inside.

"We've no choice."

We searched every room only to find furnishings playing spooks underneath white sheets blanketed with dust, but when we came to a circular consulting room it looked like I imagine it did when its owner was practicing here. On the desk an envelope was propped against an unlit candle. I made Herbert comfortable and then picked up the envelope. "This paper feels new." I started to open it until Herbert said, "Someone's here. I can feel it."

Footsteps coming straight towards us interrupted further talk. The consulting room had no windows or other exits. I had let us get cornered, and as much as it galled me all I could do now was wait and improvise.

A tall, brawny man with brown hair stepped into the room and blocked the door. He appeared young but struck me as old. His skin and gray eyes had a lackluster cast to them that "pale" doesn't accurately describe. He had handsome features and I deduced he was a laborer or used to be. The stranger recognized Herbert, who recognized him, but I couldn't tell which one made the other more anxious. There were no introductions. The stranger just asked Herbert in an odd high-pitched voice: "Why?"

I didn't understand the question and Herbert opted not to answer.

"Did you read the letter?"

"Not yet."

A pause, then the stranger repeated: "Why?"

I still had no idea what the man wanted to know, so I couldn't understand why Herbert suddenly looked a bit humbled, almost chastised. "I know you won't believe this, but my intentions were for the best."

"You meant no harm, Doctor?"

"No."

"So why not stop? You had to see the horrors you were making. Why not stop? You couldn't have thought you could ever make things right."

Herbert had trouble finding the right words, then settled on, "That didn't matter. I couldn't stop trying."

"Really? So then I suppose you never thought that a dead man might want to stay dead?"

"That's ridiculous."

"Is it? I drowned myself. Why would I want to come back?"

Herbert jerked. "You're no suicide."

"Oh, yes, I am. I was working alone on a bridge. As alone as I was in the world. I'd had enough. I let myself fall. I did my part. All you had to do was leave me dead."

"I didn't know. No one did." Herbert sounded sincere.

"Would that have mattered? You couldn't stop. Worse, you didn't care. You abandoned me."

"Not true! We thought you burned in the fire."

"I was more alone than ever! Wandering without the strength to die a second time. I never found that courage again. Then the Major came and gave me purpose. He gave everything like me purpose."

Whatever that meant got the better of Herbert. His chagrin vanished, incinerated by that indefatigable fire. "Yes. I'll never forget that night."

"And I bet you wanted to die, but you couldn't. The Major saw to that. How did that make you feel?"

"Like you in some ways, I imagine. Does that make you happy?" The stranger opted not to answer. "So what now?"

An unhappy grin sliced the stranger's lips. "Now it ends. My task is about done…I've asked you everything I've ever wanted…so why delay it?"

This was the first thing either of them had said I was pretty sure I understood. "No! Don't try it!" I needed to give the stranger a chance to change his mind, but he took one step towards Herbert, then a second, much faster than the first.

That cinched it.

Only fools visit graveyards following nightmares unarmed, and I'm not stupid. Gunfire draws attention, so I whipped the stranger's Adam's apple with a blackjack as he passed me. He clutched his throat and dropped to his knees. Killing a man is never pleasant and best for all if done quick, so I drew my stiletto, finished my task, then cleaned the knife on the back of his coat and used it to open the envelope, hoping for some answers about what was happening. What I read only rattled me more. "This letter says, 'Do with it what you will,' and it's signed 'Sir Eric Moreland Clapham-Lee, late.'" I sat and then stared at my companion. "I need answers."

"Are you sure about that? It's a long story. One you might not want to hear."

"I just saved your life! *Twice* if you count the cemetery! So don't pussyfoot unless you want me to leave."

"No, Levi, don't." He took a breath. "I will tell you all I can." But first he asked, "What do you suppose he means?"

"Who?"

"Clapham-Lee. What does he mean 'it'? Is he talking about that thing of the floor or this house of his?"

I hadn't considered that. "I suppose that depends if the note was meant for you or the dead man, don't you think?"

* * *

Herbert told me everything about his experiments in reanimation, starting with his college days to the night Clapham-Lee's tomb-legions shredded him. What started as a quest to ward away death had descended into obscenity. At the risk of repeating myself, to say Herbert West lost his way is an understatement. As for how he survived Clapham-Lee's attack in Boston and ended up in Highgate Cemetery, Herbert had no memories but did have a wonderful hypothesis.

"I can only describe it as *supranatural* radiation. Not supernatural, something beyond nature. I have to believe what I am experiencing is a part of nature, a power akin to cosmic rays that originate beyond our solar system yet can affect the Earth, or gamma radiation which can originate on our world. In either case this supranatural radiation, unlike ionizing radiation, is not biologically hazardous, but rather sustains life against all obstacles. It also appears that this radiation can be manipulated, which would explain how Clapham-Lee performed his assault on me, though that manipulation was crude at best. If I were more fanciful I might suggest this radiation is the basis for the legend of magic. But imagine what a radiation like this means to my research! This is not just a new approach; it's a virgin frontier offering limitless possibilities! And who better to blaze the trails then me, Levi? It's part of me. At times I can feel it like a heartbeat."

I won't deny that Herbert's hypothesis is outrageous, but I also find it intriguing. Its possibilities put the sideshow claims about snake oil and radium to shame, and the research will require years, maybe decades, giving Herbert and me a second chance at a productive life. Research is expensive, though, so we created Dr. Herbert to pay the bills. We also had to disguise the fact that all that remains of my new friend is his head, but for someone with my background it was a simple solution that added to the miraculous doctor's mystique. I decorated the wall and ceiling of Agar House's round consulting room with black velvet drapes, then situated a chair with a "body" behind a desk-like table in the center of the room. Dr. Herbert, "a quadriplegic," sits in this chair under a light aimed at his visitors but leaves him in relative darkness. It is a fitting sanctorum for a great doctor or great conjure-man or both, if I say so myself, and Dr. Herbert's success speaks for itself.

It might seem foolhardy to live and work in Agar House despite Clapham-Lee's potential invitation since the late Major may still harbor ill-will against Herbert, but we are convinced Clapham-Lee could find Herbert wherever he went to ground. Besides staying in Agar House gives us a high ground, so to speak, to make ready for the day if Clapham-Lee and his tomb-legions try to strike again, plus we would probably never find a better place for our research.

One thing I have not revealed, even to Herbert, is my doubt about the supranatural nature of this radiation. Why couldn't it be supernatural? Or both?

I have visited the Circle of Lebanon again several times and the trilithon is never there. I suppose because it served its purpose, but what sort of radiation has a purpose? Doesn't that suggest a conscious attribute? It may be this radiation can only exist in certain loci, much like gamma radiation can only exist under certain high energy conditions like lightning strikes. That would explain why the tomb-legions delivered that box that West had presumed contained Clapham-Lee's head that last night in Boston. The Major knew Herbert would go to an incinerator in his sub-cellar to dispose of it, which placed Herbert near the ancient masonry I saw in my nightmare. A tomb on the other side of that masonry is probably a locus for the radiation that sustained Herbert during Clapham-Lee's attack, transported Herbert to London, and somehow continues to sustain him. I also have my doubts that Clapham-Lee's head was really in that box. I suspect it is sequestered in its own sanctorum, just as I suspect what remains of Herbert's body has been sequestered as well, perhaps as trophies or perhaps to draw Herbert away from Agar House if the need ever arises.

Yes, Herbert's hypothesis intrigues me, but it also worries me. We know so little about the radiation, most of all rather it is supranatural or supernatural. What kind of force are we dealing with? Like Herbert I can't stop myself from trying to find out, so I suppose some day we will discover the good or awful answer.

ADDENDUM & ACKNOWLEDGEMENTS

Reimagining H. P. Lovecraft's weird tales into one storyline is hardly an original concept, especially since his Cthulhu Mythos stories are already somewhat allied. More than that, these and several stories written by The Lovecraft Circle—friends and fellow authors such as Robert E. Howard, Robert Bloch, Clark Ashton Smith, and Frank Belknap Long—could arguably be called the first shared universe in American literature, although the focus of *Lovecraftian* is on Lovecraft's works with only an occasional hat tip to the contributions of others. (Hey, if Lovecraft can reference Justin Geoffrey and Friedrich von Juntz, then why oh why can't I?)

I was concerned that Mr. Robert C. Harrall, administrator of the Lovecraft Estate, might not approve of this reimagining when I approached him with this idea, but, as usual, he was supportive, and for that I thank him.

My thanks also go to Eric Reichert, the late Gary Reed, and Caliber Comics. It is doubtful that this project would have seen the light of day without their faith in it and me.

Much the same can be said of S. T. Joshi, to whom this book is dedicated. Without Joshi's advice and encouragement over the years, neither this nor many of my other Lovecraft projects would exist. This book also benefited from several solution opportunities that were volunteered by Joshi.

I am indebted to Trey Baldwin for his extraordinary interior illustrations. Trey's love of Lovecraft shows in the care and detail of his artwork and it has been an honor to collaborate with him.

Further kudos to Messrs. Matthew Elliott, Rafael Nieves, and Justin Beahm for their support.

I want to once again express my gratitude to Professors J. Kenneth Kuntz and Jay Holstein of the University of Iowa's Department of Religion for teaching me so much about writing, including that most important of writer skills: how to read.

Never to be forgotten are my family, Lisa, Katie, and Jayden, who remind me that there truly are more important things in life than books and writing.

Finally and foremost I want to express my appreciation to the gentleman author from New England, Howard Phillips Lovecraft, without who *Lovecraftian* would not have been conceivable much less possible.

Until next time, dear friends.

ALSO FROM STEVEN PHILIP JONES
AND CALIBER COMICS

**Graphic Novels,
Literary Works,
Instructional Books,
and more...**

WWW.CALIBERCOMICS.COM

ALSO AVAILABLE FROM CALIBER COMICS

QUALITY GRAPHIC NOVELS TO ENTERTAIN

THE SEARCHERS: VOLUME 1
The Shape of Things to Come

Before *League of Extraordinary Gentlemen* there was *The Searchers*. At the dawn of the 20th Century the greatest literary adventurers from the minds of Wells, Doyle, Burroughs, and Haggard were created. All thought to be the work of pure fiction. However, a century later, the real-life descendents of those famous characters are recuited by the legendary Professor Challenger in order to save mankind's future. Series collected for the first time.

"Searchers is the comic book I have on the wall with a sign reading - 'Love books? Never read a comic? Try this one! ....money back guarantee...' - Dark Star Books.

WAR OF THE WORLDS: INFESTATION

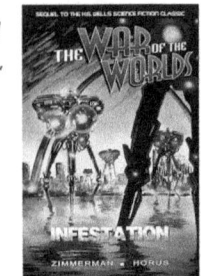

Based on the H.G. Wells classic! The "Martian Invasion" has begun again and now mankind must fight for its very humanity. It happened slowly at first but by the third year, it seemed that the war was almost over... the war was almost lost.

"Writer Randy Zimmerman has a fine grasp of drama, and spins the various strands of the story into a coherent whole... imaginative and very gritty."
- war-of-the-worlds.co.uk

HELSING: LEGACY BORN

From writer Gary Reed (Deadworld) and artists John Lowe (Captain America), Bruce McCorkindale (Godzilla). She was born into a legacy she wanted no part of and pushed into a battle recessed deep in the shadows of the night. Samantha Helsing is torn between two worlds...two allegiances...two families. The legacy of the Van Helsing family and their crusade against the "night creatures" comes to modern day with the most unlikely of all warriors.

"Congratulations on this masterpiece..."
- Paul Dale Roberts, Compuserve Reviews

"All in all, another great package from Caliber."
- Paul Haywood, Comics Forum

DEADWORLD

Before there was The Walking Dead there was Deadworld. Here is an introduction of the long running classic horror series, Deadworld, to a new audience! Considered by many to be the godfather of the original zombie comic with over 100 issues and graphic novels in print and over 1,000,000 copies sold, Deadworld ripped into the undead with intelligent zombies on a mission and a group of poor teens riding in a school bus desperately try to stay one step ahead of the sadistic, Harley-riding King Zombie. Death, mayhem, and a touch of supernatural evil made Deadworld a classic and now here's your chance to get into the story!

DAYS OF WRATH

Award winning comic writer & artist Wayne Vansant brings his gripping World War II saga of war in the Pacific to Guadalcanal and the Battle of Bloody Ridge. This is the powerful story of the long, vicious battle for Guadalcanal that occurred in 1942-43. When the U.S. Navy orders its outnumbered and outgunned ships to run from the Japanese fleet, they abandon American troops on a bloody, battered island in the South Pacific.

"Heavy on authenticity, compellingly written and beautifully drawn."
- Comics Buyers Guide

THE BOBCAT

Described as the Native American *Black Panther*. 1898. Indian Territory. Will Firemaker is a Cherokee Black-smith who is finding out that the world of ancient lore and myth of his Tribe, that Will had always thought of as tribal fairytales, are actually true and they're telling him he must replace his best friend from the animal kingdom, The Great Cat, as the guardian of his people. This sends him down a path of shock and disbelief as beings from the ancient past begin to manifest themselves in the world of reality. And as malevolent forces rise up in the wake of the fledgling Industrial Age, the future rushes head on into the Old West. Tahlequah will never be the same...

TIME GRUNTS

What if Hitler's last great Super Weapon was – Time itself! A WWII/time travel adventure that can best be described as *Band of Brothers* meets *Time Bandits*.

October, 1944. Nazi fortunes appear bleaker by the day. But in the bowels of the Wenceslas Mines, a terrible threat has emerged . . . The Nazis have discovered the ability to conquer time itself with the help of a new ominous device!

Now a rag tag group of American GIs must stop this threat to the past, present, and future . . . While dealing with their own past, prejudices, and fears in the process.

LEGENDLORE

From Caliber Comics now comes the entire Realm and Legendlore saga as a set of volumes that collects the long running critically acclaimed series. In the vein of The Lord of The Rings and The Hobbit with elements of Game of Thrones and Dungeon and Dragons.

Four normal modern day teenagers are plunged into a world they thought only existed in novels and film. They are whisked away to a magical land where dragons roam the skies, orcs and hobgoblins terrorize travelers, where unicorns prance through the forest, and kingdoms wage war for dominance. It is a world where man is just one race, joining other races such as elves, trolls, dwarves, changelings, and the dreaded night creatures who steal the night.

CALIBER
C O M I C S

www.calibercomics.com

FROM ONE OF THE PREMIER INDEPENDENT PUBLISHERS

CALIBER COMICS

GRAPHIC NOVELS • COMICS

DIGITAL BOOKS • NOVELS

WWW.CALIBERCOMICS.COM

www.ingramcontent.com/pod-product-compliance
Lightning Source LLC
Chambersburg PA
CBHW081328090726
47907CB00010B/2412